snake the Gypsy

Mikal O'Boyle

Black Rose Writing

www.blackrosewriting.com

ISBN: 978-1-61296-224-5

PUBLISHED BY BLACK ROSE WRITING

www.blackrosewriting.com

Printed in the United States of America

Snake the Gypsy is printed in Palatino Linotype

Cover design by David King @ www.kingsizecreations.com

A special thanks to my husband, Adrian O'Boyle, and my brother, Mitchell Minarich, for their endless encouragement to finish this book.

Also to my mother, Michelle Minarich, and my brother, Michael Minarich, for adding their special touch to the illustration.

Finally, a huge thank you to my father, Robert Minarich, for being that driving force that impelled me to pursue my writing career. I appreciate your determination for my success.

snake the Gypsy

Introduction

Please don't ask for my name because I simply will not tell you. It is too much of a painful matter. I can see that you are foreign and therefore can not possibly understand the complexities of the name my nation has given me, but my past is a very sad story, and if you will humor an old gypsy woman and her boy for awhile, then I would take great pleasure in telling you my life history. You see, gypsies inherit the talent of storytelling, adding color and sparkle to their stories, and no matter how implausible their stories may seem, a gypsy can make it completely believable by the emotions she expresses. Why, I have altered my story numerous times, changing it to satisfy the wish of my listeners who have never been so heartless as to walk away without dropping a piece into my collection can. I touch them, you see? We gypsies are known for telling captivating tales, and it is a gypsy's secret to know what kind of stories will delight our listeners. We can see into the windows of your soul and grasp from them your passions as well as your fears. Ah, yes, *fear*. Here is an ancient secret every gypsy learns from childhood: Fear is the most vital ingredient in any tale. We know that you

Hûvelles will concentrate wholly on the horrifying parts, remembering that image for days, weeks, years, or possibly your whole life. You aren't thinking of running from me now, are you? I have not yet told my tale, and you do not yet know what my story will be. Perhaps it will be sadness, or maybe love? I have never cared for tales of romantic grandeur as I believe love is simply an illusion, but be it so, I've learned through telling hundreds of tales that love is a very powerful ingredient indeed. I have also learned, however, that though love may posses you temporarily, it does not threaten you or summon surreal nightmares that scar you. Love is powerful, yes, but fear is the seed of hysteria. Don't ever forget that.

The Locé

As a child, a gypsy girl spent, or rather wasted, her youth on laborious days of dance lessons. It was our custom. The new generation of young females had to learn the trick of the trade that gypsy women were infamous for. They were to perform their best dance at our bi-annual festival. Men and women from all villages, those whom my nation called *Hûvelles*, would endure extensive travels to witness our festival. This is because it was put on every six months, which is a long time to wait for such an unforgettable show. When word got out that my nation was to arrive in a specific location, *Hûvelles* would flock to the nearest hotels or family residences, all in the anticipation of the *Unique*. Us gypsies were not the distributors of this title. It was the *Hûvelles* whose impertinence gave them false reason to think they had any right to call it so. They derived this title from the once-in-a-lifetime opportunity to see it. Once the festival had taken place in a village it was never to be convened there again. But the title *Unique* is a disgusting word to say since it is not a word in our language and so forces us to make weak attempts to pronounce it. It is harsh sounding, awkward, and dirty so I shall make no mention of that name anymore. From now on I will refer to it as the *Locé* because that is the proper gypsy word. I make no mention, however, of my nation's title under the very conditions of secreting my own.

The *Locé* was the biggest event of every gypsy's life. It was what they lived for, and essentially, it would determine how much money they would have to live by for the next six months. There were plenty of activities for the *Hûvelles* to experience, but for the gypsies, there could only be one trade per person. Cooks, tailors, fortunetellers, musicians, magicians, and others. Less heard of trades such as spider training, tree bending, moon shiners, fire manipulators, and sometimes when Maurice the Mover was around, floatation sessions would hold a tent at the *Locé*, but nothing-*absolutely* nothing could attract more *Hûvelles* than the dance stage. You must understand, the magic put on by a magician is only illusion, but the magic a gypsy girl performs when she dances is real. It draws you in. It makes you hungry, but most importantly, it makes you poor! Most *Hûvelles* know to walk the food tents before they see the dance show because their money would be wasted on the latter. The tents are so many different colors. One tent may be made up of an orange patch, a green one, yellow, teal, and purple all together! Color catches the eye, you see! It's magnificent. That's why glitter, both gold and silver, is spread in thick layers upon the ground. Nothing sparkles better than glitter in the moonlight. When the *Hûvelles* leave for home, their shoes are covered in it, making them feel like they have just lived a dream; a dream where they were kings, queens, princes, or princesses whose royal feet had tread over silver or gold. It is part of the allurement us gypsies specialize in.

Ribbons of all colors and materials are draped overhead so that the *Hûvelles* can walk below while admiring the arrangement of cardinal lace with burnt orange polka-dotted cottons and cat's eye green sheen silks. Mirrors, mostly circular with beveled, baroque frames, are placed around the whole *Locé* so that every form of light including the stars, the moon, flames, and fireflies are reflected in every nook and cranny of the festival. I remember once a little girl checked her reflection in a small hand-held mirror with an intricate rose detail weaving in and out of the handle. Her dress was powder purple with white lace around the bottom hem and around the sleeves. It fit her like a glove. She pulled her hair back, stuck a flowery weed behind her ear, and lit up the mirror with her smile. A few ribbons that had fallen from the hanging wires were tied around her wrists and neck. A white lace rested gently against her neck while strips of speckled denim and frayed fuchsia nylon were knotted in beautiful bows around her tiny wrists. Two tails of the lacy white dangled down her back, tangling in a couple of her brunette strands. The fireflies thought it would be sweet to perch in ideal positions within her hair to make her glow. She was a lovely little girl. I envied her.

Of course there is far more to be seen at one of our wonderful *Locés*! The music is performed and orchestrated by instruments and creatures you would never dream of! Mushrooms are used as drums, blades of grass are used as harmonicas, acorns shells are used as whistles, and even yucca seedpods are used as maracas. The musicians are usually a band made up of what we call the Ginkgos. They are the young clan of orphans in our nation who make their homes in the trees. There is something very odd yet very fascinating about them since they squat like frogs, speak in a different tongue composed of clicks and gurgles, and paint their faces to match the shape of the leaves. Considering we are vagrants, the type of trees changes often and so must the leaves on their faces. Whenever we move to a place with no trees, they find solace in the shrubbery. It is the job of the Ginkgos to tie hundreds of lines just above the strings of ribbons from one end of the *Locé* to the other. Then, to add more of a glow to the night sky, the Ginkgos hang firefly-filled lanterns upon the lines. More of these lanterns either swing from a pole outside of the tents, or they rest on the ground near the entrances so that the *Hûvelles* can find their way in, though the smell of the foods usually lures them. *Hûvelles* know their appetites, and it's up to the gypsy to entice it. Among the wide variety of foods, you can find ant kebobs, elephant trucks on a stick, scorpion skewers, sliver skivers, ostrich eggs, and if you're lucky, popper jiggies. I, myself, have never tasted a popper jiggie, but the smell drags me to the door every time it's been made. I'm shooed from doors, however. I'm not welcome in my own nation except to be a child to point a finger at. I am my mother's single child. A dirty, nameless *Girl*.

The Dark Marvel

Unfortunately I was an illegitimate child parented by a nameless mother. My shame was thrust upon me when I discovered the source of her moniker: *The Dark Marvel*. Unwittingly I called her *Marvel*, adopting the ridicule name-calling my nation took pleasure in, but she showed no contempt for the name coined by *Hûvelles*- a very specific *Hûvelle*, in fact, my faceless father. His one gift to the world was to impregnate my mother and leave her to the judgment of my merciless people. A gypsy was not to intermix with the *Hûvelles* under any circumstance with the exception that the *Hûvelle* resign his life in the village and commit himself to the life of the gypsies. Once this oath is made, he is no longer to return to his former life as a *Hûvelle*. Despite the strict decrees of my nation, my father bound himself to my mother, promising her the world and a life unknown. His promises were only good for the latter, and I remained a life unknown.

It is only through hearsay that I gained this much information, and yet some more. My mother was judged the most graceful and artistic dancer of our people. It is said that when she spun on her toes, the wind twirled around her, pulling everyone in like a cyclone. When she sprung across the earth-stage, the sand trailed her like dust does a falling star. Her curves seemed to move opposite each other, giving the illusion of a snake or some spineless creature. Her hair would bounce with every hop and caress her heart-shaped face. But I stop here with the goddess's charm. It is her face that appealed to the *Hûvelles*, enticing them to empty their wallets in her leather purse that lay at the front of the stage. It is not from an exotic beauty unmatched or a spellbound hypnosis; it was the scarf concealing everything below her eyes that drove her admirers mad. The mystery of her face combined with the elegance of her dance was enthralling. Her eyes manifested nothing but the normalcy of those of a *Hûvelle* woman. Her lashes were neither thick nor long and would solely flatter no one when she winked if it wasn't for her scarf. She would breathe strategically, inhaling the air between her and her audience while consciously lifting her chin to exaggerate the pulsating suction of the scarf to her lips. It is said that when a gypsy woman manipulates her audience in such a manner, her heart is her own, but my mother betrayed herself. She let a *Hûvelle* sweep her off her feet while she danced.

He entrapped her with his grotesque expressions during one of her routines. It was ambiguous whether he was enchanted or appalled by her performance. His mouth would curl and fall, his eyes would squint instantaneously with a grimace, and his body language conveyed dejection. Shoulders were curved into him and hands were stuffed in pockets, but for once in my mother's life no money was being removed. He just watched her in this fashion until the very end, connecting his eyes with hers through his hateful glare. She found him that night, rambling throughout the food tents of the *Locé* and caught him by the arm. He turned with that same glare and sparked a fire within her. At that very moment she loved him. And at that very moment he loved her. But his was for a moment, and hers was for a lifetime. A *Hûvelle's* favor was never so resistant towards her before, and she demanded his admiration. This assured him that my mother's vanity was her weakness, and knowing this he exploited her to his advantage. Though he indulged in nothing less than embezzlement, physical pleasures, and being the envy of every *Hûvelle*, there was nevertheless one thing he could not abuse, and that was the secrecy of my mother's scarf.

He begged her, neglected her, scorned her, and beat her. Throughout all this torture never once did he attempt to pull it off himself. His authority over her would be known by her submission to him, so he continued to antagonize her. Eventually he thought of wooing her, holding her in his arms under the starlit sky, and for the first time ever he told her he loved her. She had heard it a million times by millions of *Hûvelles*, but he executed his tone perfectly and followed it up with gentle lovemaking. She lost all sense when lying in her predator's arms and removed the scarf, exposing her disfigured nose and jaw. You see, as a child, she was hated by the other children for her perfect dancing and endless praise, so they threw a bucket of scolding water at her face out of pure jealousy. She had hidden her mutilation from that day on until this night of naive hope. His hand shot up to his mouth and he roughly shoved her off his arm. Quickly dressing himself, he gave her one last grimace and one last glare to remember him by. She replaced the scarf that he passionately spit on before he had kicked dirt in her face and walked away. That was the last time she would ever remove the scarf. She didn't cry or mourn; she only rubbed her hands on her stomach after feeling her heart skip a beat- the sign of an evil premonition.

A Dream perhaps

I remember days when I could barely walk because my toes were so bloody or my feet were too sore. My legs would cramp up at night and my back would ache intolerably. Even though I was six years old at the time, I had the appearance of an old woman, hunched over and holding my back while I dragged along at a slug's pace. My mother was full of sympathetic encouragements, my favorite being, "You are all intact, aren't you? There is no blood or bone showing! Just stretch your muscles a bit and we shall begin again." By the time the sun was up she was hovering over me, shaking me violently, and scurrying about our tent as if the apocalypse was coming and dancing was my only prayer. But I was driven by the competitive spirit that all gypsy women possess, and knowing that other girls were being roused from their sleep as well, I trudged into this daily routine and learned what was expected of me.

"You will be better than the rest," my mother would exaggerate. "I have something special in mind for you!"

At the time the lack of a name didn't bother me. My nation simply, with the literal meaning of the word, called me *Girl*. I thought it the most beautiful name in the world until childish innocence abandoned me at the age of thirteen, and I was hit in the face with the intentional simplicity of the *Hûvelle* word. I wasn't an individual. I didn't have a name that distinguished me as so and so's child. No, I was simply *Girl*. My mother's shame was a stigma upon my existence, and so the children of my nation imitated their parents like little monkeys following me, harassing me, and even physically injuring me. They would mock me and sing my alias in a hateful rhyme while sticking out their tongues. After morning dance lessons I would ramble about the nearby forest, but upon returning, the children, specifically a boy name Rockel and his sister Sorcha, would throw stones at me. My mother would only tell me to ignore these childish games my *friends* played and wash up for dinner. I noticed she never would look directly at the welts on my arms, legs, and face.

"Lift your foot, tap it lightly, slide it across the sand, swing your hips, and flip your hair." All of these instructions would come from my mother who played a quick tune on her wooden flute. All the other women played on homemade drums, but my mother refused to be like the *others*. I despised these long lessons. Mine lasted longer than any of the other girls, and I watched them run to the forest from the corner of my eye while my mother shouted more corrections at me. "NO! Hop, spin, kick, then slide! If you want to be like the others, then join the *Hûvelles!* Your blood is tainted with theirs anyway!" She would throw her flute down and reenter our tent, ignoring me the rest of the day. I would feel guilty about being half *Hûvelle,* and like any child I tried to make amends. Never once did my mother accept or even acknowledge my apologies.

I distinctly remember one night my spirits were low after a warning of abandonment from my mother. I was now thirteen, and being so young, my only resolution was to wander about aimlessly. Eventually I found a small pond close to the entrance of the forest. My mind was fixed on running away, though I had no idea where to go-another sign of a gypsy. So I squatted next to the pond and waited for some noise or some monster to pull me under. Instead a distant frog croaked, and a mosquito left a red bump near the bruise on my neck from a rock thrown by Sorcha. It was much too late for the other children to be running around, so feeling secure, I lay on the muddy banks of the pond, ruining the new dress my mother had handmade for me. I turned on my side to throw pebbles into the water, which rippled the smooth surface. A big gangly spider was forced to dodge the waves and glide across the pond towards me. At least twenty others trailed it in a straight line expanding and compressing their legs in rhythm with one another. The lead spider stayed in the middle while the others circled it then stopped all together. None of them moved until the frog croaked again. At the sound of the croak, every one of the spiders spun in a circle around the middle spider like a rehearsed dance. Leaning in closer to assure myself that I wasn't dreaming, I splashed some water on my face to prove that I was in fact witnessing this miracle, and then I climbed up onto a nearby rock and continued to watch.

Glowing lights from underneath the water's surface swam below the spiders, following them in every motion and throbbing with a yellow luminosity. The spider in the middle was frozen, spotlighted by a glowing creature beneath it that was ready for its move in the sequence. For a long while it was immobile until a symphony of frogs and crickets composed a melody in time with the rotating spiders. Suddenly, the croak of a frog similar to a bass drum plaintively boomed a waltz, initiating the movement of the middle spider. First it slowly twirled by itself, and then it twisted in a tight spiral that gradually enlarged until it reached the circling spiders. After weaving in and out of the circling spiders for some time it finally chose a partner to share the limelight with. They leaped over each other as the circling spiders changed into the formation of a star. The tune was melancholy and lingering, patiently drawing out every beat until the two partners progressed into the next movement. I had never seen such a sight in my life, and I had lost all awareness of the world. I watched every second of the waltz until the two partners met in the middle. They moved close then darted away from each other for some time before finally embracing the other with their two front legs and twirled. The little V's in the water that trailed their twelve free legs made a kind of pattern that reached the circumference of the circling spiders who were now weaving in and out of each other. I couldn't take my eyes of the two partners who maintained a tight embrace. I wanted to be part of the dance. I wanted to understand what was going on, but just as I was thinking that, the two middle spiders pushed away from each other and departed the circle reluctantly. The exit was slow and dramatic. In order to let the partners through, the circling spiders ceased their weaving and remained in a quivering circle. After the two had crossed the barrier, the glowing creatures under the water went black again, and the music of the forest stopped. Even the frogs quit their bellowing croaks.

I waited for the second show, though still in disbelief of the unimaginable, but they didn't return. Lifting myself up from the large rock, I wandered back to my mother's tent awestruck and spellbound. I fell into my bed without thinking about removing my filthy clothes and submerged into a dreamless sleep.

Mikal O'Boyle

King of Diamonds

I didn't wake up in the manner you may have imagined. There were no words of disdain or any violent shaking. Instead I woke up to a sharp and penetrating pain that pounded above my foot. I shot up and grabbed my swollen ankle blindly while trying to wipe my eyes free of dry mud. I could hear the sound of forceful smacking landing all around me on my cot. Something climbed up my back, slid over my shoulder, then stopped so that half of it was on my back and the other half lay limply on my chest. I froze as the thing curled back up towards my face, resting just short of my neck.

"Get up! Get up!" My mother shrieked. Forgetting about the throbbing pain in my ankle, I swung my legs off the side of my cot and attempted to stand up but fell helplessly onto the ground with an earsplitting scream. My mother couldn't be disturbed from her mission. She threw all the sheets off my cot, and dropping to her knees to search under it, she looked at me with a fierce expression asking, "What have you done with it?" I couldn't answer. The pain had sucked all my breath from me.

"I told you to get up!" Crawling over to me, she grabbed my elbow and jerked me to my feet. Every other step was like banging two sharp rocks against the inner and outer side of my ankle. I shouted worthless cries of protest, but she dragged me outside and let me collapse to the ground. It was only then that I noticed the frying pan being held above her head in a striking position. It was her choice of weapon. "There was a snake in your cot! I saw it crawling over your legs when I walked in this morning. Purple diamond snakes are a sign of bad luck!" After lecturing me a little longer, she turned to me with a bit of spittle on her chin and widened her eyes to a monstrous size. "Don't move!" she whispered. With the frying pan lifted in both hands and ready to come crashing down, she tiptoed in my direction. I was terrified but assured she wouldn't dare hit me with the pan. My ankle was surely an accident.

Whack! She hit me right across the middle of my back where my spine juts out the most. As I withered and curled with the fresh smarting of my injury, I felt the thing crawl down through my dress and under my leg. Its white slit eyes peeped at me beseechingly. I thought of nothing but preventing my mother from being the murderer of the snake and rolled over to stop her. "Mother! If you kill this snake I will forever rid you from my existence!" My lips became motionless except for a slight twitching. Never in my whole life had I spoken to my mother with such a tone. It was liberating.

"What did you--"

"Don't touch the snake."

I was glared at with a quizzical and terrified look. Neither of us knew how to handle my demand, as both of us were unaccustomed to any such thing. After some minutes, she dropped her arms to her side and turned to enter the tent.

"Get up. You will still learn to dance today. Don't think your sour attitude will get you out of that." I was left in the dirt with the snake approaching my face. All nine diamonds adorning its back glittered in the light of dawn and undulated when its body slithered. The slits in the front of its head were dotted with a faded green pupil that moved left and right under a milky white film. It ejected its tongue three times before ascending onto my chest and sat up as straight as a king towering before me. Its underbelly was speckled with gold. The rest of its scales were a dusty silver.

"Why did you cause me so much trouble? Maybe you do bring bad luck." I certainly didn't expect the snake to answer, but he seemed to be listening. I examined his body since I had never seen such a creature in my life. When its eyes met with mine, I watched the dim green pupils bob up and down, which reminded me of the spiders from the night before. Without knowing, I had smiled, but the pupils in his eyes vanished, and all that was left was my reflection. I looked at myself smiling with great discomfort. Suddenly I felt as if I was meant to shed the skin that was clinging to me. It felt so dirty and useless.

As soon as my mother returned, the snake slide off

me, but I noticed that his pupils had reappeared. It didn't escape for the forest like I had expected. In fact, it stayed very close. I tried to stand up, though I could only stand on one foot, and shift my weight to one side. My back was bent in a crooked fashion and would be for the rest of my life. Without sparing me one look, my mother began the tune, and I stumbled through my routine. I knew all the steps, executing each one correctly in an awkward hobble. The snake was coiled at a safe distance from my mother, swaying its head in time with the flute's tune. It watched me attentively. When I finished, my mother set down her flute without lifting her head. Her voice was soft and hollow. "One more time for today, and then you may go soak your foot in the pond." Before I could thank her she began her tune again, cuing me into motion, only this time the snake became part of the show. It slithered between my feet, weaving in and out and climbing around my body. It seemed like he thoroughly enjoyed riding the waves of my arms. When I hopped, it squirmed quickly then barrel rolled under my feet. When I preformed my serpentine move, it copied me, exaggerating its own slithering. We danced in harmony with each other as if we had practiced the dance together from the very beginning. My mother pretended not to notice, but she ended the tune abruptly. "That's enough for today. Tomorrow you will learn the end. Now go rest your foot." I limped in the direction of the pond, and upon turning around, I was glad to find the company of my diamond back friend. From that day on, we were inseparable.

Mikal O'Boyle

Prey of the Green-Eyed Monster

For the next two weeks the snake accompanied me while I polished up the grand finale of my dance. My mother had become much more despondent except for an instruction every once in a while. Though I basked in the absence of her insults, I was heartbroken with her negligence. After all, I was a lonely girl who was teased mercilessly by her peers, and now I had a mother who refused to even glance my way. During this time of social isolation, I grew very close to the snake, taking it with me whenever I went for a walk. At first I hid it from the other children, but upon catching a glimpse of its purple diamonds, they made sure to stay at least twenty feet away from me. From that distance they could only throw objects at me, but I was an impossible target when I entered the woods with its closely-knit trees. I took sanctuary in the snake as he became my protector, my shield, but most importantly, he became my friend. It sounds strange, but I could talk to him in a language I had created, and though I longed for him to utter something in response, he never did. He was a snake.

After that mysterious night at the pond, I often returned to it hoping that the spiders would come back and perform their show again. Time and time again I was disappointed. The snake always came out with me, coiling himself on the rock that I had sat on. His eyes never left me, but I never felt like I was being watched. It seemed more like he was trying to understand me, or did understand me, and had recognized me as a friend, too. There were times when he shot out at my mother whenever she came near. He hissed with an eerie rasp, which I had never heard from a snake before. Mother took great heed of the snake by remaining at a safe distance from him and using soft tones when she spoke to me. She could never get near me since the snake slept on my chest at night. I didn't want to upset my mother though, so I would practice my dances alone out by the pond sometimes. Again the snake would follow me, watch me, and even dance with me. One time a gypsy girl was spying on me when I was unaware, but the snake lashed out at her before she had the chance to throw a stone at me. I laughed uncontrollably when she screamed and turned to run like the devil. Whenever the snake thought there was danger nearby, he would slither between my feet, and other times he showed his affection by rubbing gently against my ankle. Because he was so good to me, I tried to hide the pain that all the dancing caused, but the training became more intense as the *Locé* edged nearer.

The last week of training was very difficult. My foot had healed completely though it was left slightly warped, and as I mentioned before, my back never straightened out after the frying pan incident. I had perfected my dance and even mastered the vanish-behind-the-scarf ending that my mother swore would make me the envy of every gypsy. Even I was surprised by the perfection of the scarf trick. My mother's talent hadn't left her old bones, and I was very grateful that she was teaching me the secret of the trade. It was moments like that when my mother showed her love for me. I was too young to comprehend the love-hate conflict that she had with me, but unfortunately, it was hate that usually prevailed. When the last couple of days before the *Locé* had finally arrived, she spent most of the hours pampering me. She shone like a pearl in the sea, but the reason was unclear to me. I attributed it to all the excitement of the Locé. I even worried about her. I had never seen her in such high spirits, but eventually her excitement rubbed off on me, and I shared her flowing energy.

The day had finally come, and I was ecstatic to be in my first Locé instead of watching from around the corner of a tent. Women were dressed up beautifully and painted their faces so as to resemble some earthy element, and then they would step on stage to perform their dances without fault. The level of elegance and entertainment in their dance determined the amount of money they would be rewarded. It became a competition of who could earn the most money. Of course the money being rewarded was a prize given by the seduced men in the audience, so vanity had something to do with the heightened competitive spirit as well. After my mother had retired from dancing some years ago, the winner had always varied. I had it in my mind to change that.

I sat stiff and mute upon the chair as my mother painted my face like the reflection of a starlit sky. My skirt that she had made reached down to my feet and covered my disfigured ankle. It was a midnight blue with bits of silver glitter sparkling on the material like stars in the evening. Upon my torso I wore a formfitting white long-sleeve shirt that stopped mid-drift in order to show off my flat stomach. No matter how I moved, the shirt clung to my feminine curves. The wide neckline clung around the outside of my shoulders to compensate for the amount of skin covered by my skirt. It looked seductive without trying too hard. The grand finale scarf, intricately woven so that an image of the moon was hidden when it was wrapped around my waist, was otherwise a light blue that complimented my skirt. The snake sat coiled in the grass nearby, watching as my mother prepared me. When my outfit was complete, he nodded his head, which I secretly took to be a sign of approval.

When I finally looked down at my body I realized that

I had become a woman. I had an adequate sized chest that I was, until then, unaware of. My brown hair flowed about my face after my mother had washed it and curled it at the tips. It was a complete transformation into a woman I had never been before. My confidence swelled in my chest, and I was ready to dance at once, but my mother signed me up to be the sixteenth of the twenty-five dancers. At first I threw a stubborn hissy fit about my positioning, but after my mother explained her reason, I was impressed by her clever thinking. The first group of dancers was observed by a small handful of *Hûvelles* who arrived right on time, and the very last dancers entertained the small amount of remaining *Hûvelles* who had too much to drink and had lost the time and their money. Therefore it was a strategic move to place me in the middle so that the crowd of *Hûvelles* would be thick and still enchanted with the *Locé*. Only after I had made a name for myself could I then be the last dancer. When I was so good that every *Hûvelle* would wait until it was my turn to dance before they considered leaving, then I could be the last dancer. But for now, I was a rising star and had to be patient with my success.

The stage was occupied by dancer number ten and my boost of excitement had settled down before turning into a distracting anxiety. I decided the best way to cool my nerves was to go for a walk around the pond. I placed the snake on my shoulder like I usually did and headed towards the entrance of the forest. The snake, without warning, shot down to the grass and began slithering between my feet. He hissed his raspy hiss, which terrified me. I knew something bad was approaching, but I didn't have time to react. Suddenly, a hand covered my mouth and a knife pressed its blade against my neck.

"If you dare scream, I will slit your throat." Rockel pushed the knife tighter against my skin, cutting into it slightly. I didn't notice that the snake had squirmed his way back up to my neck.

"I've heard about the great scarf-ending you've learned. Sorcha was spying on you one day and was very upset about your performance. She's worked too hard to lose to a nameless ghost like you. We all know who your mother is, and her disgraceful past, but the product of a scandal will not ruin my sister's future. Do you—*OW!*"

Rockel threw his knife down and grabbed his hand. Two little fang marks oozed blood from their holes. Without waiting to see what he would do, I turned and started to run, but Rockel was much stronger than me. He caught up to me, threw me on the ground, spit on my face, and then struck me so hard in the head that I lost consciousness. When I woke up from the darkness, I found I was trapped in a wooden box and couldn't move. I thought it wise to stay quiet and wait for something to happen. Foreign voices of men floated around me, and I had never yearned for my mother more than I did then. I had no other choice but to lie in the box and wait naively for a happy ending.

Mikal O'Boyle

The Ancient

Tree

The exhaustion of fear had put me to sleep temporarily, but I was rudely awakened by a rough shove. I was still in the box, but it banged so hard against something outside that it woke me up with a throbbing head. My back ached insufferably. I felt my heart flutter in my chest with panic. It seemed like I was suffocating and couldn't scream even though I wanted to. I could see small streaks of light through the cracks of the boards, but it didn't pacify me. Then it accrued to me: I didn't know where the snake was. I desperately needed his company and protection. He had to be in the box somewhere. I didn't feel anything move. My panic blew up into terror. What had happened to the snake? And where was I?

A foreign voice filled my ears during my moment of horror. It seemed to be a man shouting for someone named *Jankins* to give him a hand, and soon I was being carried by, I assumed, two men. To control my heart, I tried to focus on their voices. It definitely wasn't Rockel.

"What is in here? Isn't it supposed to be some bottles of wine? Do you hear any clanking?"

"No, Mr. Jankins. I don't hear nothing. Maybe we should set it down and make sure we wasn't cheated."

I came down hard with a thud and was scared that the two men would find me and think I was responsible for the missing wine. I held my breath and shut my eyes. I heard the crowbar being shoved under the boards, a few nails being pried out of the wood, and then I saw the light of the sun through my eyelids. It relieved me somewhat.

"What's this? Who are you and what happened to your mug? Where's the wine?"

I shook my head in sheer horror. The man's face was alien to me being half covered with prickly stubble and half covered with dirt. His skin was badly burnt by the sun, and his few teeth were a deep shade of yellow. I could barely stand his breath. The other man was very brawny and well groomed. His muscles were large and impressive. By the softness of his countenance I felt that he was a little less savage. He spoke with a calmer voice.

"How did you get in there lass?"

"Don't go off spoiling her Mr. Jankins. She's a criminal, and criminals are punished with death." The other man, who had just issued the threat, glared down at me with a vengeance. He gave a quiet growl, which silenced me.

"Shut up. She's a young girl. Let's hear what she's got to say for herself." The clean-shaven man who was called Mr. Jankins bent over the box with his hands on his knees.

Mikal O'Boyle

He didn't exactly smile at me. It was more of a smirk of amusement. I stared at both the men wide-eyed. My jaws were clamped and my body was paralyzed. The brutish man scratched his greasy hair before saying, "It be no use, Mr. Jankins. Cat's got her tongue, so it has. It wouldn't be right to have a lass on the ship nohow. Bad luck. And she's already disappeared the captain's wine. We caught her red-handed. Who else could of took all them bottles?"

"You're right Bren. Bad lack is the worst possible thing for a crew. Just let her go. Don't want any blood on our hands when we're about to sail. That's worse luck than finding her. I'll buy the captain some more wine. Besides, the captain will have our heads if he thought we were the ones who lost his wine."

Bren scratched his head like a confused ape.

"Huh. I didn't think of it that way."

They didn't take me out of the box before they swung it back and flung me out. I rolled hard against the rocky shore, cutting my arms and face. Blood was everywhere on my body, staining mostly the sleeves and neckline of my top as well as an area high up on my skirt. My thighs felt sticky and were smeared with blood. Pulling off the dry seaweed that clung to me, I noticed a purple diamond under the raveling of my light blue scarf. I picked the snake up gingerly, but its body hung lifelessly in my hand. The snake was dead. Its head was angled to one side. I never knew if Rockel, the box, or the hard rocks it landed on inflicted its death, but I knew I hated everyone fervently. I bound it up in seaweed, tied the scarf around him like a bandage, and then threw him onto the boat when the crew was on break. I hoped with all my heart it would bring that ship bad luck. I wanted the whole crew to drown in a storm.

Cupping water in my hands, I washed off the paint and blood from my body. My legs and stomach ached as I stood up to walk, and my hands were shaking terribly. I tore my shirt and wrapped my cuts with the shreds before heading off in any direction. There was no point in trying to figure out where I was. The world seemed new and dark to me. As I meandered through the village, *Hûvelles* stared at me disapprovingly, shaking their heads or squeezing their children to their sides. I made faces back, shouting incomprehensible mumblings in my snake language so they would think I had cast a curse on them. My amusement didn't last long before an Hûvelle's husband struck me down. I decided then it would be best to walk the path of shame quietly.

As I passed through the village I came to a forest. It was something that always seemed like a home to me. I sought refuge under the big shady leaves and selected a humongous tree with twisted limbs to rest under. It had a scent of earth to it, and I guessed it had to be an ancient tree by the width of it. The bareness of its branches didn't quite deteriorate the tree's majestic presence. I leaned back against the bark and tried to find the sun through its canopy of leaves, but my thoughts soon went in a different direction, and I couldn't stop myself from crying. My body shook violently, and my chest ached from gasping for air. I tried to suppress my pathetic whining, but it was no use, and the forest echoed with the sound of a dying creature. It didn't matter; no one was there to mourn me. It wounded me to think my mother would feel no loss at my disappearance, and I began to scream louder. I stifled myself with my dirty hands, smearing mud all around my face. After calming down for a few moments, I fell asleep uncomfortably between the roots of the ancient tree, dreaming of nothing but the purple diamond snake. When I woke up I was tortured by the reality of his death and my loneliness.

Or so I thought.

My hair began to rise off my head without touching it, and the sound of crumbling leaves being pulled out of the tangles crackled in my ear. I jumped back and turned to see what was touching me and found a boy about my age squatting by the tree, twirling a leaf in his hand. He had a strange smile on his face. I couldn't tell if it was condescending or friendly. Standing up, he said something in a different language that was more like a soft breeze hitting my face, and I smiled stupidly as I shook my head to indicate that I hadn't understood him. My stomach turned with the look he gave me, a face so ugly and so sinister it was neither of gypsy or *Hûvelle*. His eyes changed into a deep green and his teeth, once normal, were now very sharp. He frowned with a fury and climbed up the tree with great agility and speed. The abnormality of his movements convinced me I was still dreaming until a hand grabbed me by the hair and pulled me up into the mass of dying leaves. Before I knew it, I was surrounded by hundreds of these demon faces, including the boy I had seen before, who was now closing in on me, licking his lips with a blue salivating tongue.

The ugly Boy

There was nothing left to do. I thought I was done for so I closed my eyes and prepared for the pain of being eaten alive. I screamed from the sharp pang of teeth entering my arm. The teeth ripped out from my flesh, and my scream was overtaken by a horrendous growl.

"She is not a *snattal*. She is human!" The voice that had spoken these words was very deep and very nasty. It sounded like it was in pain when it talked. The words sort of wheezed from its throat as if it was gasping for its last breath. The noises he made didn't encourage me to open my eyes.

"Who brought her here?" The thing speaking was obviously enraged, but I thought my life might be spared.

"I did, Kruss. I was deceived by her dress. She seemed to be a *snattal* in human form. I was on watch duty and--"

A mad roar vibrated the whole tree. Something screeched and whined like a beaten dog. For a second my heart went out for it, but then I remembered that horrible face.

"You dare bring this tasteless human into *my* kingdom! You dare to take the first bite before me, your king, and forget that my servants starve?" There were a couple angry snorts and a wicked laugh before he continued. "You shall hang for this. Lish! Orro! Tie him to the blushing branch! Make sure to use the poison oak rope. We shall see who starves to death first!"

At that moment I wished I had covered my ears. The begging, the cries, the despair that poured out from my predator was heart wrenching. I couldn't help but whimper slightly. It sneaked out of my lips. I felt a long, sharp nail drag a strand of hair out of my face. Breath that reeked of rotting fish blew in my direction. I could feel myself shaking, but my eyes still stayed shut.

"And just what were *you* doing knocking on the door of my palace?"

It was the one called Kruss who was speaking. The one who had sentenced the other monster to the blushing branch, whatever that was. I couldn't find the courage to answer him.

"Speak, girl! It may save your life."

The mentioning of the name Girl invoked a thousand memories of my nation. I missed my mother, I missed the forest, and I missed the snake. I began to cry when the thought of my diamond back friend crossed my mind, but the image of him gave me some strength.

"I was looking for my friend." The trembling words fell from my lips.

"And what does your friend look like, girl?"

His voice was a little more threatening and suspicious. I thought the innocence in my answer would win my freedom.

"A snake with purple diamonds."

Kruss inhaled quickly. I could feel the shock in the room. I wasn't even sure how I was in a room considering I was in a tree. The grip that Kruss had on my hair tightened and pulled. I didn't dare protest. He began to hiss, but it wasn't anything like the snake. It was more like that of a spatting cat. I didn't know what I had said wrong. All I knew was that even with my eyes closed, I could feel the monsters staring at me. Kruss leaned in close to my face so that the smell of rotting fish made me sick to my stomach.

"I shall take great pleasure in planning your death. When I capture the enemy lord, I will make him watch. He will feel your pain in addition to the pain of losing his fellow filth of *snattals*. I will make sure your journey to death is long and painful. A friend of the diamond back is a traitor to this kingdom. You shall die like a traitor."

I didn't have time to recover from my terror. A large paw of some sort grabbed a load of my hair and dragged me off. I refused to open my eyes until it felt like I was alone, but now my thoughts were consumed by fantasies of my horrible death. Doors were being pushed open in front of the monster that was dragging me. My hunchback banged against what I assumed to be some stairs. I screamed out in pain once, but I was silenced by a hard smack to my mouth. The stairs seemed to last forever, and so did the pain. If I couldn't handle that, then how I was I going to handle an endless journey to death?

snake the Gypsy

Finally the stairs ended. Another door was flung open, and I was roughly thrown into a wall before the door was shut again. I waited a few minutes but didn't hear anything. I decided to open my eyes for the first time since I saw that ugly boy's face. Maybe they were a mutated form of Ginkgos, but what was a *snattal,* and how could they change from human to monster? The ugly boy's face kept creeping into my mind, so I tried to think of something else. The room I was in was circular and extremely small. It had been carved out of the interior of the tree. The door could be discovered by the lines that traced its frame, but there was no handle on my side of it. Other than that, it was hard to see because it was camouflaged within the wall. I began to feel the surface of my prison. It was very smooth and polished. There was no light in the room except for the hole about forty feet high that I had for a ceiling. Through it came the sunlight of the afternoon. There wasn't much else to the room except for a small picture of some sort carved in the floor. I couldn't tell what it was, but it looked like a little man with a crown. Something had run its claws over it, which made it hard to distinguish. I looked for anything else that might keep my interest, but there was nothing. I knew that if I stayed there long, I would lose my sanity before I lost my life, which was beginning to sound like a better alternative.

Mikal O'Boyle

Healing Fangs

How had I gotten myself into this position? I tried to think back to how I wound up in a tree prison with monsters who wanted to eat me. I couldn't focus very well on the answer as my arm where the ugly boy had bitten me was burning with pain. I looked down at the teeth marks and winced as there was festering skin around the puncture wounds. It looked as if it was foaming. The veins around it began to turn a deep shade of purple and spread down my arm like the nervures of a leaf. Some of the purple tendrils were stretching across my collarbone and targeting my heart. I would have panicked only for the thought of dying there and then seemed like a pleasant thing. Then the thought of turning into one of the monsters was too much to bear, and I screamed over and over again. The pain of the wound was heavy. It burned, ached, throbbed, and felt like my skin was being ripped apart. Even when one of the monsters came sweeping in the door, I continued to scream.

The sight of the monster was worse than the pain in my arm. He looked like he was part human, part spider, and part monkey. Four long fangs hung out of his mouth like razors. They were salivating with blue goo. Two fire orange eyes looked at me with disgust. He moved towards me on all fours like a monkey would, repeatedly licking the dripping blue goo from his lips and sucking it off his fangs with a sickening slurping sound. His skin was fuzzy like the fur on a big black tarantula. I nearly lost my stomach when he ripped out one of his fangs with a furious howl and let some of the inner yellow fluid plop onto my wound. In an instant, there was relief. Within moments, the wound had healed completely and the pain had stopped. I turned my head to thank him in hopes to make a friend from an enemy, but he had already spun around to leave. When he departed the room, he didn't move like he had before. This time he scattered out frantically like a spider. His arms and legs were bent outwards, and his body was low to the ground in the middle. The door shut behind him, and I was alone again.

Briefly I thought that my eyesight had left me, as I couldn't see any of the sunlight. The room was very dark, and only a dull light lit up the circular walls. When the moon shone high above me, I realized that the pain I had suffered from the bite was so intense that I had lost track of time. It was now evening, and the moon was following its routine path. As my eyes grew heavy with sleepiness, I feared that it may have been venom from the monster's fang taking an effect. I saw a very familiar face looking down upon me from the high opening, but when I looked again, I saw a blur of leaves and was convinced that a branch had swept over. Tiny shadows on the wall began to wiggle like worms. The moon was angled so that its beams fell only on me and left everything else to my accelerating imagination. The little worms began to whip their bodies furiously, flicking and lashing like they were suffering excruciating pain. I felt my breath quicken. There was some kind of havoc happening around me that I didn't understand. What was wrong with these worms? They started to fall off the walls and onto the ground by my bare feet. I drew my knees into my chest, paranoid that they may try to drill holes into my skin or under my toenails. At first only a couple fell and bounced around helplessly, but within a matter of minutes, they all began to fall from the walls. The worms that fell were instantly replaced by more worms that burrowed through the prison wood. A million holes appeared in the circular wall, all of which were widened from penetrating worms driven by some contagious rage. Suddenly more worms tumbled from the opening above me. They plopped like raindrops into my hair and tried to dig deep into my scalp. I shot up off the ground, shook my head and body, and jumped up and down, but the worms kept coming. Soon there was a pool of them up to my knees. Squirming, wiggling, flicking their bodies, the worms worked their way up to my neck. I was stuck in a quicksand of worms. All I could do was scream, and that's all I did. I cried, struggled, and screamed as loud as I could. Just as the worms reached my nose, a sheering pain raced over my upper arm, waking me up from my terrible nightmare.

"Shut your dirty mouth before you wake up the whole

palace!" The monster with the salivating fangs snarled at me before leaving me again to my troubled, hallucinating mind. His hideous face had been inches away from mine. I could smell the fresh kill on his breath. Hopefully it had been an animal and not a human. His eyes were radiant orange with a white pupil that reached out towards the eyelashes in a bunch of slender spokes. The effect was like a spider web. I didn't look at anything else but his eyes. If his fangs were to puncture my skin again, I didn't want to see it. His eyes were so marvelously bizarre that they were enough to keep my focus. I was glad, however, that he chose not to bite me. I wasn't sure how to survive this tormenting imprisonment. The best solution seemed to be to stay awake, which was easy now that I had a gaping wound on my upper arm from the monster slicing it open with one of his elongated claws. I wondered if this kind of cut would initiate another strange phase of hallucinations, but after awhile nothing happened. Eventually my eyes began to force themselves shut. I couldn't help but give in.

By the time I awoke the following day, the sun was high above me, indicating that it was close to midday. A tray of what must have been food was already injected into my room through a slot I hadn't noticed at the bottom of the door. It was well hidden by the uniformity of the smooth wood. I wasn't sure about touching any of the food I was given. I examined it first, smelled it, inspected the color and shapes, and moved the plate to see what kind of solidity it maintained. I wasn't satisfied with any of it. The colors were moldy green and rotten brown.

There wasn't a single thing on the plate that I recognized except for a burnt acorn, which I wouldn't be quick to define as food. I turned my head away from it in an attempt to ignore it, but my stomach lurched out in protest. I hadn't eaten since the morning of the *Locé*. I couldn't tell if my stomach wrenched from the sight of the food or from hunger. No matter how hard I tried to take my mind off the plate, I continued to feel my eyes betray me. From my peripheral view, I sneaked a peek or two at the food, and then shot them back up at the sun. A few seconds would go by, and my eyes would be lured to the plate again. Finally I gave in.

With great reluctance I picked up the biggest thing on the plate. Even the texture of the thing was slimy, mushy, and incredibly gooey. It was green, almost yellow, and looked like the body of a slug. Blue goop hung from it like syrup as I held it up before my eyes. There was nothing else to do but close my eyes, open my mouth wide, and slurp the slug-like food down my throat. The taste was surprisingly tolerable. It had a familiar taste, but I couldn't put my thumb on it. I waited for a horrendous pain to burn in my stomach, but nothing happened. The rest of the food was looking adequate now that the dull ache of hunger had been teased. It took less than two minutes for me to down the rest of the food. There was a couple of red raisin-looking things which were kind of rough to chew, an acorn which proved to be shockingly tender, a few crunchy leaf-like chips, and two more of the slug blobs. All of the food was covered in the blue syrup that seemed to add a savory taste to everything.

My stomach was certainly grateful for the replenishment. I was just rubbing it when I felt a tingling sensation on my arm, and when I looked, I was shocked to discover the cut from the monster's claw was suturing itself. Never had I seen a wound heal at such a rapid speed. It was like the two split sides of the skin were pulling in towards each other until they attached and molded together so that there was no trace of a cut. Pleasantly surprised by the sudden turn of luck, I laid back in the noon sun and dozed off, but not for long. The door opened and in came the monster guard. He collected the plate, sniffed it, and then grunted. For hours he was gone. My stomach pains began to creep back up on me again, and I nearly lusted for the blue goop. Finally the monster returned, but to my dismay, there was nothing on the plate. Instead, the monster was chewing food right in front of me to taunt me. Or so I thought. In an awkward movement, the monster raised the plate to his chin, opened his mouth, which was missing the fangs, and let the gum-mashed food slide out onto the plate. The blue goop was everywhere. He hadn't been chewing the food; he had been swishing it around in his mouth to cover it in his blue fang serum. Instantly I felt my throat contracting and my jaws tense up. I swallowed as hard as I could and fought back the rebelling vomit. At that moment, I decided that my death would be due to starvation.

Mikal O'Boyle

Rakata Morbido

There is no pain worse than that of starvation. Even the permanent hump on my back and twisted ankle was no comparisons to the shrinking of my stomach. Weakness drained all energy from me. I was tired throughout most of the day and night. The only way I could find any form of comfort was by laying in fetal position with my arms crossed over my stomach. I cried silently to myself for fear of the monster's cutting claws. I had lost track of how many times the sun had come and gone, but it didn't matter anymore. Who in the world would come to rescue me, and if they did, how would they find me? I had a few more grotesque hallucinations and three more blurred glimpses of that strange face-like branch hovering on the edge of high opening. Every time the branch swayed over the opening, I mistook it for a face, and my hope flared up until I realized that the same branch had mocked and duped me yet again. The monster guard outside my door reached me before my hallucinations caused too much commotion, and he had even taken a small interest in my fasting, but didn't seem too concerned. He left the same plate there for days. I was relieved to think he would leave me there to die, but I was wrong.

For the third time that day, the door had opened. It usually opened about twice a day for a lunch and dinner check. A familiar voice filled my ears with as much venom as the monster's bite.

"Get up! You die today!"

It was Kruss. The sheer ecstasy in his voice was bone chilling. I didn't move. If he wanted to kill me on the spot, then I would make it easy for him.

"I said get up, you worm!"

A swift kick to my shoulder made me moan with agony. What was worse was the mentioning of worms. I may have been hallucinating again, but I could have sworn that Kruss's toes had turned into a bunch of wiggling worms. That was enough to get me off the floor. I pushed myself up with a surprising amount of strength. As I straightened myself out, I realized I wasn't in as bad a shape as I thought I might have been. The loss of time and long days of sitting alone had made things seem much worse that they were. I was still famished, but much more alive than I had figured. Kruss didn't appreciate the look of confidence on my face, so he leveled up to me and hissed. For the first time, I saw the face of my executioner. His fangs were sharper than the guard at my door and much larger. They were completely covered with blue saliva. Both his eyes were glued to mine but with a very intense glare of intimidation. My eyes narrowed in on his spider web pupils that were shaped like the guard's, only Kruss's eyes were black with red spokes extending out from the center. I fell back slightly from the horrid smell that emitted from his mouth. I braved a long look at his demonic face, but when his nose rose in a satanic scowl, I couldn't look on.

"Snake lovers and *snattal* allies are worthy of one death. A slow one." He laughed menacingly before saying, *"Rakata Morbido."* I had no idea what he said, but I felt myself shutter. The thick hatred packed in those two words nearly knocked me over when he said them. How could I have brought this upon myself? The snake was only a friend—a comfort. I didn't know he was a great rival to something as demonic as these monsters who capture and torture innocent gypsy girls like myself. Despite all of the traumatic misfortunes I was subject to because of my friendship with the snake, I didn't regret it. He did die because of me after all.

With one incomprehensible word from Kruss, the monster guard grabbed a load of my hair and dragged me out the door, down the stairs, along an infinite corridor, and into an empty room save a wooden table. Upon this table he threw my weak body before binding my wrists and ankles with some sort of unbreakable vine. The way my twisted ankle was pulled caused immense pain. I gasped out for breaths to calm my panic, but it didn't work. I focused my eyes on the darkness of the room, which I wish I hadn't done. Hanging above me like a hundred bats were a crowd of monsters all anticipating the glorified kill. Kruss was speaking to the audience in a language I didn't recognize. Every once in awhile the crowd would sputter out sounds of excitement. I picked out the words *Rakata Morbido* a couple times from his speech in which the sputtering noises from the audience would directly follow. All I could see was an insurmountable number of inhuman eyes swaying back and forth like a pendulum as they watched Kruss pace the floor with his arms above his head, overcome with joy. I could see nothing of the tree's interior because all of the monsters were crammed together and wiggled about as if they were the worms from my nightmares. Eyes of all different colors honed in on me, and although all of them gleamed with a dull glow, none of them were bright. Some of them flashed in the newly torched light held by the monster guard. Seeing the shine on their eyes reminded me of hundreds of cats in the night. I could make out mossy green, slate gray, molten gold, and marble white. I wanted to faint when all of them snapped on me simultaneously with a hungry greed. Not one of them expressed any concern for my life.

"Now, snake lover, for centuries your ally has been destroying us one by one. My own brother was devoured by those purple back *worms*." I shivered at the last word. The monster reveled in my terror. "Now you shall squirm just like them. This will not end quickly nor will the pain subside. *Remember* that when the first phase begins." At the word *remember* the audience cackled and spat like fighting alley cats. I took it to be laughing. "This is going to be deliciously satisfying." Kruss threw his head back, jerked his body as if he was having an epileptic fit, and then dropped his chin to his chest. His eyes had grown twice in size, and the colors of them had vanished. They were replaced by a small light barely visible though glimmering from somewhere deep within his skull. The eyelids had rolled back so that their undersides were revealed. He gave a devilish smirk, which presented not one, but three sets of fangs. The front fangs were dripping with the blue goop that the monster guard had. The second fang was oozing a darker blue goop that sizzled on the floor when he drooled. It seemed to be acidic. The last set of fangs weren't covered in anything slimy. At the tip of them, however, was a black stain. It looked like they had been dipped in some kind of ink. The fangs that were showing were more terrifying than the presentation of torture tools I had once seen used in France. The victim at the time had felt the function of each one in order of least painful to most excruciating. Now I would feel the power of this monster's fangs.

In went the first fangs right into my arm where the former cut wound had healed. My body immediately reacted negatively to it. My limbs went weak, my stomach turned, and I was severely ill. My head ached with fever and I began to sweat. I tried to roll to comfort my stomach but it was no use as I was tied down. Every muscle in my body was on fire. All of this happened slowly, one after the other, as if I was becoming more and more sick. The pain worsened for hours while the monsters watched with great joy. I moaned out with utter disgust at the upturning of my stomach and was answered by Kruss's elated smile.

I screamed in between each groan and wanted to clutch at my exposed stomach, which seemed to be turning inside-out in front of all the monsters. It was some time before Kruss went in for the second bite. Two fangs were inserted just below the first two holes. A burning itch started at my toes and deliberately worked its way up my body. The urge to scratch was fierce. While the yearning to assuage the itching in my feet nearly consumed me, I was reminded with every beat in my chest of the throbbing pain the first bite was causing. I wiggled violently in the binds to try to free my hands and scratch at my feet.

Despite the overwhelming fatigue in my body, I fought. After an hour had passed, the itch was up to my ankles. With each dragged out hour, the itch climbed higher. The more I struggled with the vines, the more I rubbed my wrists and ankles raw. My bad ankle was beyond hurting. As the itch moved up to my knees, my toes burned as badly as if they had been set on fire. I whipped my head to the right to see if the monster guard was still holding his torch, and he was. My head swung back into the upright position on the table, and the eyes of all the monsters were blurred into a massive smear of dark colors. They burst out in their metallic-sounding laugh. I could feel blood dripping down from my wrists as I continued to rub them against the vine. I wasn't aware of the thorns on them. They ripped into my flesh. After having screamed more in one hour than I had in my entire life, an intense exhaustion overwhelmed me and probably would have caused me to sink into an unconsciousness only for the torture that was prying my eyes open. When the itch reached my thighs, the burning sensation was up to my shins. I thought I was being burned to death, but there was no fire. My throat was unable to make any more noises after all the screaming I had done. It was very sore. I tried to scream anyway and brought about more pain on myself. Once the itch had reached as high as it could go, the burn was my main problem. An invisible fire was incinerating my body. I almost made myself believe I could smell the burnt flesh. It was revolting.

I couldn't focus on Kruss's face anymore. Everything was in fast motion. My eyes fluttered as rapid as the wings of a hummingbird. I could make out a blob leaning over me with two white posts falling towards my arm. The bottoms of the posts were black, but I couldn't think of anything else but mud. That's what it had to be. I felt the pressure of a thousand tons on my arm. Something remarkably heavy had crushed my elbow. A rabid growl stuffed my ears. It echoed over and over again. The heavy pressure was lifted from my arm, which was a great relief despite the fire that was devouring my body and disintegrating my bones into ash. I remained in this delirium of pain for what seemed like an eternity. The fire had finally reached my mouth with flowing lava that spilled down into my throat, chest, and stomach. All I could do was scream one last time and hope that Death would hear my call.

Hayden

For a second, I thought my scream had caused an earthquake. An aggressive tremor had thrown my body into a kind of seizure, but that was far more tolerable than the excruciating burn, which had instantly cooled into an uncomfortable chill. Even though the sudden iciness felt like a symptom caused by a bad case of influenza, I could feel myself breathing again. Each breath brought refreshing air into my withered lungs. Finally, the burn had ceased completely and the itch was easing up, too. My hearing had come back to me, but the chaotic screams where not very comforting, and I felt myself cringing with fear whenever one of the shrieks of agony surged through me. They were different than anything I had ever heard before and lingered within me. The last thing to come back was my eyesight, which cleared up a face that I did not recognize. It was the face of a handsome boy with a worried expression. Behind him was that blurred branch that seemed to be following me. When I squinted my eyes to see better, the branch was gone and the boy was smiling. I thought I had died.

I opened my mouth to say something but my voice

had gone entirely. My throat was raw and sore. It hurt to try.

"Sh. Don't speak. I will explain later. First we'll get you out of here."

With one scoop of his arms, the boy lifted me up without any difficulty. The pressure of his bicep squeezing my arm as he carried me made me feel incredibly small. His other arm was wrapped under the back of my legs, and his hand tightly gripped my knee. I had never felt so safe in my life, but there was one stubborn thought that kept haunting me. It was telling me that he could be another one of these monsters in a more convincing disguise as a boy. I rested my swollen eyes on his countenance, such a face that I will never forget. Even in the fuzzy mosaic picture that my poisoned eyes allowed me, the boy was a very welcoming sight. I couldn't tell if he was aware of my admiration, but as he swept me away from the torture chamber, my hearing tuned into a scuffling sound blowing into the hellish tree from the windows. The entire tree shook violently, knocking the boy and myself to the ground more than once. When his arms loosened to regain his balance, my arm slipped from his hold and crushed a pile of leaves with a fragile crumbling noise. At first I thought I might have shattered my feeble arm, but to a gypsy, the sound of leaves was easily recognized. All of the shaking and wind must have caused the leaves to scatter everywhere. Apparently they had blown into the windows of the tree and created a kind of crêpe-paper floor.

Snake the Gypsy

All the excitement rushed to my head, making me dizzy with droning noises and unsteady sight. Large blobs of green dropped from somewhere above me with terrifying screams. Then there was complete darkness for some long minutes, and finally a full beam of light and warmth. It had to be the sun. In the natural light, I could make out the falling shapes a little better, although I wish I hadn't watched. The big blobs of green were enraged monsters falling, flailing wildly, from the branches of the old tree and landing rigidly on the roots below them. None of them got up. They must have died on impact. Other things, things that I couldn't comprehend, were bursting in the air with small showers of gold glitter like tiny fireworks. It seemed like birds or some sort of giant insects were exploding in mid flight. The confusion of the falling monsters and exploding bursts of gold pushed me over the edge with vertigo. I held on with all my might to the boy's arms, which had reached down for me again, but an unexpected kick from a monster slammed the boy to ground, flinging me into a large root. I hadn't the strength to get up. All I could do was roll under the root and watch the boy and the monster wrestle on the ground before me. I desperately wanted to help defend the boy. A great passion flared within me, and I managed to throw a fallen torch holder at the monster. It hit him square in the back. He wailed then left the boy to come finish me off. He dug his catlike nails into my hand and twisted them in deeper. Just as the boy did, the monster lifted me up effortlessly, raised me above his head, and hurled me into a nearby lake. He screeched with laughter as I panicked for fear of being too weak to swim. I splashed helplessly, but my head sunk beneath the surface. I held my breath, waiting to drown.

My chest began to ache, demanding me to breath in air that was not permitted me. I kept my mouth closed, refusing to make my death come sooner than it should, and thankfully so because just as the pain of drowning was beginning to subside into an eternal numbness, my mouth was forced open by the same hand that had been holding on to my knee. It was the handsome boy, with a look of concern distorting his face into an even more wobbly vision. As my eyes were still refocusing, I caught a glimpse of another green blob with two white smudges emerging from the bottom. The boy must have seen the terror in my face because somehow, with great skill, he lowered me gingerly to the ground and with those same gentle arms, he spun with unfathomable strength and connected his fist with the green blob. I didn't dare watch as the boy put an end to the unlucky monster. His maddened movements were too similar to that of the monsters', and it frightened me. I was determined to keep my eyes closed until the sounds of death were gone. Not putting up a fight, I allowed this boy to carry me away, assuming I was going to be the entertainment for another kingdom of monsters. But instead he ran swiftly for quite some time until he stood before a massive tree, much like the last one, only this one was smaller and had leaves of green trimmed with gold. Its branches sprouted from everywhere giving it a full and lush appearance. I felt a bit revived as I was presented to the tree. One of its larger branches reached down and curled around my stomach, rolling me up half its length. The branch then released me over a circular opening in the bark, much like the opening to my previous cell, and I fell in the darkness for a couple of minutes. I thought it might be another prison to keep me in, but the fall lasted for quite some time. Finally I landed gently onto soft slope and glided down with speed. I slid for a at least five minutes before I shot out of a hole and right onto a silk sheet spread laid over a wooden frame. In a matter of seconds, I was greeted by the seemingly omnipresent boy who had hopefully rescued me. He smiled.

"Are you alright?"

"I've been bitten." I couldn't remember where I had been bitten, so I turned my head and let him examine me.

"I'll take care of that."

With some kind of dewy salve, he smothered my arm in a place that was sore, though I hadn't been aware of the pain until he had rubbed it. I looked down to see if there was any sign of a bite, and I nearly jumped out of the bed with panic. Discolored veins pulsated under my skin like giant worms. Purple, green, and red tendrils had crept their way up my arm, around my shoulder, and over my chest. Each tiny tendril was outlined with a thick black. I was disgusted with the sight. Red splotches dotted my entire body, but I could see them begin to dissolve. The bright purple, red, and green that flowed in my veins were slowly retreating back to where the teeth fang had left a scar. The chill was letting up. I watched the boy continuously rub his hand over the fang marks until the symptoms had drastically improved. When he was satisfied with the recovery, he placed a grass that looked like it had been chewed up and spat out over the fang marks. The scent was a fusion of lemon and mint. The boy smiled awkwardly at me.

"What's your name?" I noticed he couldn't make eye contact.

"I don't have one." My answer caught him off-guard. He was even more embarrassed, though I didn't mean to make him feel that way.

"A nameless child? Where are you from?"

"I can't remember." Now it was my turn to be embarrassed.

"Then the symptoms are effective. The Goblin venom has an amnesia poison in it. Don't worry, you will regain your memory within a day. Do you know of the Goblins?"

"I have never seen one in my life before this."

"If only it had stayed that way!" The boy stood up to go, but feeling more awake from the aroma of the remedy, I blurted out a couple questions myself.

"Who are you?"

"My name is Hayden, but I will save that story for another day."

"Where am I?"

"Poor girl, you have stumbled into the most disastrous battle imaginable. This is the tree of the Fairies, as I'm sure you are well aware of, and you have been rescued from the Goblins. The tree they reside in now was usurped by a traitor Goblin king, Kruss, who pretended to be an ally of our beloved Fairy king centuries ago. Our Lord's son was sovereign over the ill-fated tree until Kruss slaughtered the prince and reigned over the Tree of Fairy Lords ever since. They have caused terror among the Fairy people, swallowing them, baiting them for fish when caught in their natural form, releasing a slow working poison into them, or other such tortures." He paused for a second and smirked. "I'm sorry. I imagine you know all about the war well, but hearing of the Goblins and seeing them are two different things. Your father and mother obviously have kept you very secure if you were unable to recognize a Goblin, but then again, their disguises are very deceptive. Now that the Fairies have taken a stance, the Goblins grow hungry, which is why an innocent Fairy like yourself was captured." The boy's eyes slowly connected with mine for the first time. I could tell he was monitoring my reactions to his story.

"The first Goblin knew you were a Fairy masquerading in human form, so he took on the form of a human as well to trick you into thinking he was also a Fairy, but you were clever enough to pretend that you didn't speak our language. Unfortunately, he knew you to be a fraud and brought you to be slaughtered in their tree. You were undoubtedly going to be eaten, although half blood is not as preferred as pure Fairy blood."

His words stunned me. I didn't understand anything

he was saying. "I'm not a Fairy, nor am I a *Hûvelle*. I am a gypsy. Well, have gypsy." I'm sure he was surprised to hear my response, but I was equally surprised to hear him imply that he and I were Fairies.

"Your words are foreign to me. But you can explain them at a later time. You need to rest or the medicine will not take full effect. You will forget parts of your history if you do not sleep now, so please try to close your eyes and rest."

He left me in the disbelief of my condition. There were no such things as Fairies or Goblins, was there? And war between the two seemed ridiculous. How could little Fairy people, known so well in ancient stories, defeat Goblins who were cruel and ten times their size? Then again, Hayden was taller than me, and stronger by considerable lengths, and *he* was a Fairy. Or was he? These questions filled my head for at least two hours before I felt a strong exhaustion overtake me. I began to close my eyes, but just before they gave in to the heavy pull, that blurred branch appeared in the corner of my room. Without any ounce of strength left in my body, I closed my eyes and the memory of that haunting branch withdrew into a concealed cache in my mind.

A valuable Friend

"Wake up! Hurry!"

Hayden ripped the sheets from my body and tossed some course clothing on my legs. He was flouncing about the chamber and gathering weapons from the closet positioned directly across the bed. His arms were hugging arrows, a bow, a hook tied to a rope, a spear, and a slingshot. I watched from the bed while pulling on the clothes he had given me, though unsure of how they were properly worn, and followed him. My legs were shaky, but the adrenaline from the panic gave me strength. Hayden, however, seemed unable to cope with the frenzy and dropped an arrow without noticing. I grabbed it in silence, as I was afraid that saying anything would hinder his mad rush to wherever it was he was going. I trailed him through winding corridors with faces carved in the walls like portraits, which were framed with ivy. Many of the halls were similarly adorned with regal busts protruding from all sides. I wanted to stop and get a better look, but the corridors were designed like a labyrinth, and Hayden had already gotten further ahead of me. Every time he turned a corner I got a small glimpse of the back of his shirt, and by the time I reached the corner, he was turning another. I tried to sprint, but my legs were running on emergency energy.

Finally, I cut around one last corner and found Hayden standing, childlike, with all the weapons sticking out from either side of him, before a grand entrance to a bright room. The height and width of the door was remarkable. I could see Hayden's unruly ginger hair standing out against the intense light coming through the entrance. A yellowish light spilled through it like a cave as Hayden hesitated before the mouth of it. It seemed as if he finally decided to move forward, but he tripped on the long shaft of the spear and tumbled into the opening with his weapons spilling everywhere. As he scampered to collect his fallen armory, I thought of a young boy who had broken his mother's vase and was trying to collect the pieces before she saw it. The poor guy was in a jumble with his oversized velvet shirt getting in the way, so I jumped forward to help him, but as the light from the entrance hit my face, I could do nothing except stand dazed while twenty pairs of golden eyes scrutinized me from head to toe.

Twenty little men the size of my hand glared at me. Their eyes were expressionless, and their mouths were hidden under a cotton-like beard. Forty golden eyes stared

Snake the Gypsy

at me without blinking. The rest of their body was
enveloped in a kind of fog. I couldn't decipher whether
they walked or floated. I must have appeared outlandish,
standing sheepishly with both hands gripping the arrow
and my hair, which was in a disheveled mess on top of my
head. Half of my face was obscured by my hair, and the
other half was burning. A table separated the tiny men
into ten on either side, each with a plate of fruit in front of
them. Some of the fruits I recognized, but others were too
exotic or oddly shaped. Wisps of wind bustled around the
room like a thousand butterflies fluttering past my ears. I
looked down at Hayden who was moving his mouth as if
to talk. I shouted his name so he would hear me over the
wind. I felt like I was standing in the eye of a tornado, but
eventually the fluttering stopped. Hayden turned to me
with a somewhat contemptuous look on his face. His eyes
were a dazzling green even though they were not pleased.

"You shouldn't interrupt the Lords when they are
discussing matters in need of immediate attention." He
was brushing his shirt downwards. I looked down at my
attire and blushed with mortification. I was wearing
something that resembled a burlap sack.

"I'm sorry, I didn't hear them talking." I brushed the
loose hairs away from my face.

"I wondered why you didn't answer them when they
asked for your name."

"They spoke to me?"

His voice became rushed and impatient. I felt like I
was doing everything wrong.

"Yes! Could you not hear them? Are you *not* of our people?" His question was sarcastic, but I didn't catch that.

"You mean a Fairy?"

"Yes! Of course! What else would I mean?" He whipped the bangs out of his face. The boy had changed completely from the first time I had met him.

"I told you, I am a gypsy. Well, half gypsy."

"And half Fairy."

"No, I have no Fairy blood in me."

Hayden's face screwed up into an expression of pure horror. He closed his eyes tight and grimaced as if he was in pain, and then he freed one of his hands and slammed it against his forehead. It slid down his face, dragging the skin below his eyes and his bottom lip. He was being a little too dramatic. I had done nothing wrong.

"Oh no. OH NO! I thought you were from a foreign forest!"

"I am. From many forests actually. We move around a lot to perform our *Locé*, but I was--"

"Be quiet. Let me think!"

Hayden cleared his throat, lifted his head to the Lords who were waiting patiently, and opened his mouth. Again the wisps of wind started, and I realized then that the sound of the wind was the sound of their voices. He ended his speech with a low bow, but one of the lords shot up so fast that he knocked down his chair behind him. His words came out like a booming thunderstorm. His face was red with fury, and he looked at me in disgust with eyes of scorching gold. When the storm ceased, Hayden nodded and led me out of the room by the elbow. I was scared of what he was going to say.

"I am very sorry to have brought you into this. You are now a prisoner of the Fairies."

I couldn't believe it. I was completely innocent.

"A prisoner! What have I done?"

"A human or any other creature outside of the Fairy world is not to witness the secrets of the Fairies, and you have trespassed upon sacred territory. The Lords' domain is a private meeting room suitable only for Fairy eyes. You have seen too much already and must live the rest of your life in our dungeons to prevent any threats upon our people, assuming you are a Goblin spy. Please do not try to argue as it will only make your life more miserable. I will do my best to persuade them that you're an innocent and inept human who was blind to the Goblin's tricks."

"I'm not a *human*, I'm --"

"The Fairies are a friendly people, so you have no reason to fear us. The Lords are only taking precaution against Goblin spies. One Goblin breached the hidden entrance of the Fairies and poisoned Lord Yew's fruit with acid rain-- a quick acting poison that will kill Fairies. We later found the Goblin gnawing the flesh off our Lord's corpse."

I gave him a look of utter shock. He spoke so quickly that I couldn't find a moment to interrupt him, so I was forced to wait until he was done. He rushed me back down the same corridor with the carved faces etched into the wall. It wasn't until I was lead back into my room before I found the chance to talk.

"Listen Hayden. I've been through so many miseries that the fear of death has turned into a wish for death. My father abandoned me, my mother hated me, and my only friend was unjustly killed. In fact, my only friend was a purple diamond snake who would follow me around. How pathetic is that? I've been physically abused more than I can count, and my heart presses its shattered pieces into my chest with every beat. I don't care for this foolish war between Fairies and Goblins, and I would like to leave. Kill me if you must, but I will not rot in a dungeon. Let me at least die in a more romantic way."

Hayden stood in the doorway for a few minutes with a puzzled look on his face. He raised his hands to his hips and chewed on his lower lip in concentration.

"Stay here. There is something I must report to the Lords."

Without another word, he returned to the meeting room for a while, leaving me with my thoughts about dying in a dungeon. I figured it would have been more honorable to die as the feast of a Goblin than to sit alone in a chamber and wish I had the snake with me again. But it wasn't long before Hayden came back, walking on his toes in delight like a little boy. His arms shot up into the air.

"I have saved your life!"

"You've what?"

My voice was far more sarcastic than it should have been.

"I told them about your snake friend. Fairies are great

allies with the snakes and creatures of the world. Goblins eat them for that reason. However, purple diamond snakes are of the royal snake family and extremely rare to happen upon. So it is a great loss that your friend has died, but it is strange that the snake became your companion. It is rare for any Fairy or friend alike to find common ground with a human. You must be hiding something from me. Don't be afraid to tell me. It can only be good news if it befriended you with the Diamond lineage."

I shrugged my shoulders indifferently and said in a matter-of-fact way, "I don't know. We became friends and dancing partners."

"Ah, well that validates your story. The diamond lords love to participate in a good reel, but it doesn't explain why he entrusted you to his company."

"I don't know."

"Did you sing to the full moon?" Hayden clasped his hands together and held them against his chest.

"Why would I do that?"

"Did you drink the dewdrop of a newly bloomed rose?"

"No."

"Tell me, have you been pricked with the needle of a white porcupine?"

"No. What is the point of these questions?"

Hayden's lips quivered with annoyance. His hands dropped and separated.

"Everything I've mentioned is a sign of the wandering warrior who is prophesied to win the war between the

Fairies and Goblins. Perhaps he misinterpreted one of his instincts and deemed you the warrior. But that's illogical because the warrior could never be female."

I squinted my eyes at him.

"Why is that?"

At the raw warning tone of my voice, Hayden altered his tone to a more apologetic one.

"Warriors are not females. Nevertheless, you must have a pure heart because the diamond back made his presence known to you. The Lords have concurred that you are free to roam the palace, but you may not leave the tree. It is too dangerous outside in the forest, and the death of a diamond back's comrade will place a curse on our people. Their friends are to be treated most hospitably."

"So, I *am* a prisoner?"

Hayden thought for a moment, then he replied, "Well, yes."

Dancing with the stars

Three months had gone by since I had been taken prisoner by those foul Goblins. I was becoming accustomed to the new tree I was prisoner of, but it didn't feel much like a confinement. The tree was far more beautiful than all our *Locés* could ever hope to measure up to. Everything was full of life! Even the birds greeted the rising sun with a glorious aubade that woke me up like a tender nudge. I was permitted to visit only two places of the kingdom, but these two places, my chamber and the Lineage Corridor, were enough for my contentment. My chamber was located in the uppermost branch of the tree where the sun shined the brightest. It was tightly secured in a cradle of gold-trimmed leaves that curled over the exterior of my room like ivy. Oftentimes I would look outside one of the two windows and gaze at the sparking gold edge of the leaves in the sunlight. On windy days, my branch would sway slowly, lulling me to sleep. Other than that, my chamber was decorated with various petals of all kinds of flowers. They were strategically chosen so that the scents of the varying flowers complimented each other. There were multiple colors on my wall, which made it feel as if I was living in a rainbow. When the sun shone through the window, the petals lit up and stretched as if they, too, were waking up. My bed was even more of a welcome as it was made up of the cottony seeds of dandelions. When I was a young girl, I used to blow on them after making a wish. Now I was dreaming on them.

The only time I was free to explore the kingdom was whenever the army was out on a hunt for Goblins, which was very frequent. So I spent a lot of my time perusing the Lineage Corridor of Fairy lords. As I mentioned before, there were portraits of regal faces carved in the walls of the corridors and framed by the leaves of dark green foliage. Hundreds of the solemn faces stared out from the walls with eyes made from solid gold. They were very intimidating to look at, but very handsome as well. I examined them as I walked by, touching the fine features of their faces. I wanted to know much more about them, but I didn't have anyone to talk to. Hayden was constantly leading Goblin hunts, and nobody else was to be found. It almost felt like an abandoned tree except for the occasional gusts of strong winds that suggested the Lords were arguing amongst themselves again. I assumed that the battle between the Fairies and Goblins was nothing to worry about.

Being within the tree's walls made me feel safer than I

had ever felt before, and without anyone to talk to, there was no bad news to be heard. So with a leisurely mood, I continued to walk to Lineage Corridor daily. I was a bit nervous to walk along the floor when I first entered the long hallway alone. A thin layer of bark that was completely transparent stretched all the way down the corridor. Beneath this thin layer I could see water surging through vein-like channels within the tree. At first I was afraid that I might break the thin floor, but curiosity got the best of me, and I took my first step. Nothing happened. I plucked up the courage to move forward, and in the reflection of the well-polished floor I saw the ambrosial fruits that hung overhead. The ceiling was covered entirely by a thick shrubbery that produced an abundance of dangling fruit dropping down within an arm's reach. Some of the fruits hung low beside the portraits but never in front of them. There were peaches, apples, strawberries, blueberries, bananas, and every other fruit including some that were mysterious to me. I tasted them anyway, savoring the sweet or sour juices that burst inside my mouth. They were more delectable than any of the fruits offered by my nation, and I craved them for every meal. Their juices sufficed as the perfect beverage, and their meat provided the perfect food.

The usage of light for the Fairies did not include candles, torches, or fireplaces. Instead billions of fireflies drifted throughout the hallways at night, glittering about like distant stars. They would float in through the windows of the bark and blink their lights after about two hours to signal a relief shift to the other lights. Some flies would entertain themselves with a dance, swirling around each other and creating illusions of a trailing string of light. They would paint glowing pictures in the air of waltzing couples or twirling women. It evoked my desire to dance now that it was a thing of choice rather than obligation, and I spun with the fireflies. They flew around me, sometimes accidentally getting too close to me and rubbing their glowing dust on my body. Some would accidentally tangle in my hair, but they easily escaped when I stopped to breath. I hadn't realized how long it had been since I danced with so much fervor. The glowing streaks lighting up the room were like magical fireworks. A memory of the spiders dancing in the pond back home flashed through my mind. I started to feel tears slip down my face, and I stopped. My home, my nation, was only a memory now. An aching feeling of loneliness stabbed me in the heart. I was exhausted. Standing in a sweat-soaked shirt, I felt a sharp pain cramp in my stomach, and then I fell hard to the ground squirming like a worm. My hand clasped my chest as I struggled for air. My heart pounded, then stopped. There was no doubting what had happened —it was obvious that my heart had skipped a beat. Again it hit, tightening my body into a fetal position. The pain eventually subsided, and I attributed the sudden sharp pangs to the intense dance I had just preformed.

Though I had begun my dance in silence, it ended with a soft receding of a fiddle. It came into my mind that someone had been watching me, so I set out after the last note that tried to escape my ear. It turned corners sharply, banging into the walls and making a clatter. I ran as swiftly as I could after having such a painful episode, but the note was fleeting. It began to fade away, and I knew it was moving further and further from me. I hadn't paid much attention to the faces that watched me from the walls. The corridor seemed everlasting with twists and turns, but eventually I came to the end of it. The note was still in ear's reach and happily I had cornered it at the end of the corridor. Finally it leaped into an open doorway to the right, which I was hesitant to enter. I hadn't been given permission to visit any chambers other than my own.

"You dance better than any Fairy in this kingdom."

The voice and language was a warm invitation. I peeked around the door to look in. A man stood at a window with his back to me. On the chair beside him was the sleeping fiddle.

"Thank you."

"Have you been dancing long?"

"Since I was a young girl, yes."

"What has happened to your back?"

No one had brought any attention to my hunch until that very moment. I had forgotten about it myself. The shock of someone seeing me when I couldn't see them sent shivers through me. The voice sounded like it belonged to an older man. A *Hûvelle*.

"It was an accident. I fell out of a tree."

"Don't lie to me."

The voice had changed from pleasant to irritated. It

was rough and gravely.

"I'm not."

"The fireflies tell me you have been abused by a regretful mother. A frying pan was it?"

I stood with my mouth opened wide. Memories flooded back to me. Horrible memories. I shut them out before they overwhelmed me with grief.

"How do they know?"

"These delicate little things like to fly into your ear and light up your memories. They find your story to be very poignant and full of sorrow. Come here."

I approached the man who still had his back towards me. His hands pressed hard against the low pane of an opening in the wall of the tree. The chamber he was in had petals on the walls like mine, but his were wilted. Thankfully, he spoke the language of the *Hûvelles* perfectly.

"Your sorrowful story doesn't end here."

"What do you mean?"

"Those pains will continue for some time. I'm sorry about that."

"It's okay. I've grown used to pain."

"I'm sorry to hear that, too."

"Who are you? Why do you pity me? I appreciate it, but I don't need it."

"I have a name appointed by the Fairies and therefore used only by the Fairies. I'm sorry I cannot tell you. I am like you in a way. I was born and never named by my biological father. He reared me for a few years until he died at a young age and left me to raise myself, but one day I was captured by a ravished Goblin. Hayden saved me as he has saved you. Unfortunately my mother was a Goblin in human form when my father met her; much like the boy you saw twirling the leaf. She manipulated him into falling in love with her and within a year I was born." The man paused and lifted his head to look out the window. He sighed deeply before continuing. "When I was five, an unfamiliar horn blew from within the forest, and my mother collapsed in a seizure. My father laid her in bed and waited for the doctor's arrival the following day, but by morning she was gone. It was then my father changed for the worse. Finally, when he was near death, I heard a crunching sound coming from his room, and I saw my mother shredding apart my father's body with her teeth. She had transformed into her Goblin form. She attempted to attack me, but that's when Hayden appeared."

My stomach cramped again, and I was forced to the floor in pain. The man helped me up and guided me to a chair.

"I can't get away from my fate though. The Fairies are going to kill me the night after tomorrow. It's all they can do.

"Kill you?"

"Yes. I am turning myself. As the war rages on, my blood curdles and burns. I can feel the hunger for Fairy flesh and a thirst for their blood. Even the scent of you is faint, but I desire a taste. I'm strong enough to resist it now, but in a week or so I will have devoured you."

"I do not fear death."

"Don't fool yourself. You fear it. You shiver at the mere thought of being alone. You scream at the nibble of a Goblin. Don't try to convince me you are not scared. No one will shun you for your fear because there are things you have not yet seen that you should be scared of."

The man had turned to me in a fury. He had snarled his face into an ugly mask. For a moment, he wasn't a *Hûvelle,* but he caught himself before he was carried away by his Goblin side.

"How can I be scared of something I haven't even seen?"

"Your answer is the trembling of your body."

"Why are you saying these things to me?"

"Because you are going to play a major role in the war to come. You have to stay alive and protect the Fairies to the best of your ability. They are going extinct, and if the Goblins are the victors, the world, along with your gypsy people, will suffer a horrible death."

"I have no one to care for. My only friend was brutally murdered."

The man shifted. I could tell I had said something that affected him. He began to pace the floor by the window.

"Yes, the snake. You were lucky to have had such a noble friend. But all is not lost. You cannot be alone your whole life. Trust in that. And your diamond back friend saw something in you that even the fireflies couldn't shed light on. You puzzle me. I wish I could live to resolve the riddle."

The man returned to his window in silence, and I took my leave. As I walked out his door, a melancholy tuned played on his fiddle like a death egression, chilling me like the stare of the Fairy Lords.

Mikal O'Boyle

The Fleeting Moment

I couldn't stop thinking about the wretched man's misery after the night I had talked with him. I wanted to know who he was. All day I sat in my chamber, watching the leaves spark here and there in the sun, imagining that this *Hûvelle* was some kind of fallen hero. He was the only man I could talk to, and he was going to die the following night. Curiosity quickly burst into an engulfing anger. I couldn't help but think that if Hayden hadn't saved me in the nick of time, that I, too, would be persecuted the same way. If the man hadn't been raised by his *Hûvelle* father, and then by the Fairies in the following years, he would probably be part of the Goblin army this very moment. And his mother, what foul intentions she had! To have a child with an innocent *Hûvelle*, and then devour the very man who helped create her son! The heartache the father must have suffered before she first sunk her teeth into him must have been intolerable! It must have been more painful than the infectious poison. The fiddle player had said she changed at the sudden blast of a horn. What could that possibly have been? Was it an instrument of the Fairies or the Goblins?

As the day went on, I began to hate the way the Fairies treated this ill-begotten *Hûvelle*. I wanted Hayden to return and save him again, but I hadn't seen Hayden for weeks! By evening time, I found myself dancing with the fireflies again. It seemed like the only way I could clear my head. Unwittingly, I allowed myself to be hypnotized by the fiddle, dancing on tiptoes with the fireflies to the *Hûvelle's* lovely tunes. His music was heartbreaking, and I began to cry. I was very unlike myself in this state—more romantic than usual. My wild gypsy dance settled into soft heartfelt movements. Pity, loneliness, sadness poured into every twist and twirl, every bend, and every sway. The fireflies' flashes were much slower, lingering a little bit longer than usual, but the darkness between the flashes were just as long. One moment I would be spinning in the dark, and in the next moment I would be sashaying in a yellow glow. All of my movements were urged on by my dramatic emotions: fierce, daring, and foolhardy emotions. Every bound and leap was executed with a profound strength that lurched out from my gut. My arms snapped into the motions as if a puppet-master was tugging them with hostile precision. My heart pumped its beats at a pace I was unaccustomed to. I was oblivious to the carved out faces in the walls, including the face sculpted from an ivory flesh.

Mikal O'Boyle

For the first time during my incarceration, I took no heed of the things around me, and though I never had any need to keep watch with such an impregnable security guarding the Fairy Tree, I still kept a tight surveillance on my surroundings. But because the *Hûvelle's* music was so liberating, and because my situation was so easy to desert, I admit that I forgot all about where I was, who I was, and what the world was really like. All of the pressure was off of me. I danced because I knew it was what I was meant to do, and it was exactly what I wanted to do at that moment. The fireflies were unmatched as dance partners, bar the snake of course, and their lights had put me in a trance. I was pulled so deeply into the twinkling twilight that I didn't even notice that the face of ivory flesh was not a sculpture at all. It was Hayden's handsome face. Without a warning, Hayden had walked in on my dance during my one lapse of mind. He must have been there the whole time, watching me lose myself among the dazzling sea of fireflies. Just before I made a grand finish, my self-awareness came back to me, and I was surprised to find that the tune had altered from slow and sad to quick and aggressive. I was neither crying nor lonely; it was a different feeling than before.

"Well done!"

Hayden's intrusion shook me from my stupor. I was excited to see him, but I hid my reaction. My heart was already racing with passion from the dance.

"How long have you been there?"

"Thankfully from the beginning. I've never seen

dancing executed with such precision and ardor."

He seemed less like the Hayden I had first met. There was something very familiar about him. I craved this side of him.

"Do you dance?"

"Once upon a time."

"Would you like to join me?"

"With what music? It seems to have stopped. And besides, I could never match your skill level."

I blushed. I took no notice of the trickling sweat and fuming heat that was being released from my body. His words put me in a fluster, and my cheeks began to burn, but I managed to speak.

"The music will start with the first twirl, and I am not that proud. I desire a dance with you."

"Then let us dance."

The tune had turned from plaintive to sweet; bouncing with every step we took. In the darkness, our silhouettes were illuminated with the dust of the fireflies. We swept down the hallway, breathing heavily in excitement. I had no control over my emotions, being intoxicated with the romance of the music. The helplessness was almost overwhelmingly exalting. His hands, with one fully flattened on the small of my back and the other clasping my own, were yielding yet commanding at the same time. It was a sense of comfort that flushed over me; a feeling that was unfamiliar to me. My bare feet were directly in line with his velvety green shoes, and every so often, my toes brushed against his skin-tight under armor concealing his legs. He must have removed the heavier armor upon arrival, and thankfully so, because it allowed for our flexible movements. Slowly, my leg rose into the air, and in like time, my skirt slid down my slender thigh until the bottom of it rested a few inches below my knee. I arched my back over his supportive arm and breathed in as I felt his hand curve around my rib cage. I knew that my hair had fallen in a way that softened my feminine features. I could feel the constraint of my top against my chest whenever I took in a breath. Everything was so tight, but nothing was tighter than Hayden's hold of me. He easily felt the lightness of my body, and I could tell by his sharp drawing of breath that he, too, had been pulled into the trance, only this time, I was outside of my body, watching from within the vines hanging from the ceiling. I narrowed my sight on his free hand that hovered above my neck. It was trembling for fear of doing what the music tempted him to do. Slowly, with much hesitation, the hand floated towards my blushing cheek. The fingers moved up and down, as if the thought of being controlled by the music was an indulgence. They stopped just above my left ear, waiting for something to constrain him, but there was nothing to stop the divine feeling of his fingers pushing the loose strands out of my face before curling them behind my ear. My eyes, though already closed, rolled to the back of my head.

I didn't want this rapturous feeling to end, so I lowered my leg and met Hayden with my eyes for a few seconds before spinning and pushing my back into his chest. His left arm swept around my stomach, and his right hand crossed over my collarbone and latched onto my left shoulder. We swayed, just as the snake had done to my mother's flute, in one single motion. My head fell back against his shoulder, exposing my bare neck. I lifted my leg again, only this time it extended out in front of us, and all of my weight lay against Hayden. He dragged me back a few feet, and I pointed my toes accordingly. Then he leaned back and threw me into the air with a spin so that I could exchange my legs with one graceful kick and land snugly into his bent arms. My forehead now rested on his chest, which heaved heavily. I looked up pitifully at him, purposefully pouting my lips and opening my eyes wide. My hair was tossed back in a messy wave. My face was glowing with a healthy fusion of colors. Below me the water within the tree flowed smoothly beneath the transparent bark. I knew I had him. He looked down at me with wild eyes. His jaws were jutting out slightly from the tightness of his clamped teeth. I could see that every muscle of his body was tensed. Together we drew in a breath, knowing that the big moment was about to come, and in one final movement, he shifted his hands under my arms, and lifted my feet from the ground to hold me over him. I grasped his strong shoulders for balance, holding myself in a position with perfect grace. My legs formed a v-shape with pointed toes. Hayden slowly rotated as if to show our daring feat to the audience of wooden faces. Everything had fallen into place with this one perfectly executed performance. The glitter from the fireflies drenched my hair like dew drops dripping from strings. I could feel him staring up at me hungrily. I returned his look of desire and admiration, and at that exact moment, I loved him.

Then, like the discord of a snapping fiddle string, Hayden dropped me unexpectedly. He pushed me away quickly and pulled his hands in to himself. "I must be going now." His voice was quivering, and he spoke rather abruptly. I noticed that his cheeks were still as pink as mine. We both were drenched with sweat from the exertion of our dance. I quickly sweetened my voice into that of a pleading supplicant.

"But the song isn't over."

He turned his back to me, ignoring my great effort to be as feminine as possible. His voice found its command, and with a gruff resolute, he retorted in a short breath.

"It isn't right."

"You and me?"

"Yes."

"Why? Don't you feel the sublime rhythm of our dance? We were like water spiders." I spoke the final sentence without thinking.

"I have to go. I'll explain tomorrow. Please forgive me for ruining such a beautiful thing."

"Don't call me beautiful."

"I wasn't- Please excuse me until tomorrow. I will call on you."

He spun on his heel and left in an instant. My body was the only thing glowing under the fireflies. Again I was alone and abandoned. The music had ceased, and I felt my heart harden, though at the same time hope permitted me to yearn for a better explanation on the following day. I wanted him to tell me that he couldn't love me until after the battle. That he didn't want me to fall in love with a man who may die in the upcoming days. But I wanted to feel that sense of worry and fear for him. I wanted us to be an embodiment of the unconditional love praised about in every gypsy tale of the heart. If love is truly eternal, then I would never feel alone. There would be a connection between the afterworld and the living world until my time had elapsed, reuniting me with my fallen hero. A gypsy and a… what was he? It didn't matter. If he was a Goblin I would still love him. But to be alone in love is the worst isolation one can suffer. My fate was in the hands of a warrior.

Mikal O'Boyle

A Heavy Load

The sun rose to greet me. I had been dressed for two hours and spent another hour bracing myself for Hayden's speech. It was going to be either a rejection ruled by a compassionate heart, or a blunt refusal based on his disinterest in me. I trembled from fear of the latter. I had been alone all my life, but I had never loved before. It seemed to be one chance of hope, and if he crushed it, he would crush me. My happiness depended on him, and though the anticipation was rotting my stomach, the pressure of breaking someone's heart wasn't upon me but upon Hayden, and so I felt relieved to know where my heart stood. That is until it jumped at the sound of a very light knock at my door. I raced over to it, stopped short, regained my composure, and then proceeded to open the door with those same pitiful eyes and that same sweet smile. All of it came crashing down into a look of contempt as I stared back at a beautiful woman who was certainly not Hayden. How could another living thing other than Hayden possibly knock on my door *then*! What could have possessed her to be so asinine! I was in no mood to be friendly, but she whisked in past me and sat with perfect posture on the foot of my bed. Her eyes were very stony for a beautiful woman.

"You are the gypsy girl. The friend of the snake?"

Her voice was very small, but full of control.

"Yes." I was going to keep the conversation short.

"Queer."

With a quick, condescending laugh, she looked away from me and remained silent. I cleared my throat to get her attention. I wish I hadn't done so. She retorted with bitterness.

"What do you want, other than the man I love?"

I was certainly not expecting such a question. Her eyes narrowed. The angrier she became, the more beautiful she was. A glint of gold flashed in her eyes, making them appear to be on fire. She crossed her arms over her chest and glared at me without blinking.

"Excuse me?"

"Listen carefully, gypsy. You have come too late. You're seductive dancing won't work on a man who is in love with a Fairy. There is no greater being. How could Hayden possibly lower himself to loving a mere human when he has a far more superior love as mine? I am much more beautiful, graceful, intelligent, and desirable. Our love is something you should take heed not to disturb. If you should try any more foul play with Hayden again, I will personally see to it that you are forbidden from this forest. Do you understand?"

I blinked at her stupidly. No words could find their way to my mouth. I was in shock at the pretty sounding voice that spoke so roughly. I confess that she was far more superior to me in every way that she had mentioned, but love is not constricted by such trivial things as beauty. Besides, I wasn't ugly. These thoughts began to invoke feelings of hatred towards this haughty Fairy. How could she have such great authority in the kingdom of Fairies? I doubted the credibility of her words. She was all show. Now that my confidence had risen, my tongue finally dislodged itself from the back of my teeth.

"Hayden can choose for himself, can't he?"

She widened her lips into an beautifully sinister smile.

"He already has. You have no hold over his heart. He would die for me on the spot if it should so please me."

Her last words were poison to my ears. I was beginning to think she was a Goblin in human form.

"That's awfully *loving* of you, isn't it? I would never boast about the man I love dying for me. It seems a bit heartless. You may not even have a heart, but Hayden does. When my head was against Hayden's chest last night, I--"

Before I could finish my sentence, the woman's face was inches away from mine. I thought instantly that she was a Goblin having possessed such abnormal speeds, but then something truly bizarre happened. The woman opened her mouth as wide as she could and released a lashing wind into my face. Her eyes were two circles of blazing gold. I was deafened by what seemed like a vicious tornado that had made its way into my chamber. My eyes teared up from the gushes of wind that pierced them. For about two minutes I endured the storm that had attacked me, and then with a sharp smack to my face, the woman, having returned to her former state, pushed past me and out the door, which was now hanging on one hinge. My room had been torn asunder by the woman's outrageous uproar. Terrified, I tried to calm myself down by cleaning the mess around me. After about two hours, I had managed to make my chamber look a little more decent, but it was still very untidy. I sat on my bed to take a rest, and my thoughts began to turn. I had been badly scorned by a Fairy who was jealous of the love Hayden and I had for each other. Her intimidating anger was far less scary when I thought of how Hayden had brushed my hair from my face. I began to trace his defined features with my inner eye when a soft shuffling sound broke into my thoughts.

"Good morning." Hayden's head poked from around my broken door after a light tapping. He didn't seem to notice that it was hanging from one hinge. His eyes were dark underneath and sad.

"Good morning to you, too." The Fairy woman's threat had faded from my mind that moment I saw him. He stepped in, looked around at the mess that was left behind by her, and then continued.

"I had prepared a speech for you, but when I entered your room, I completely forgot it."

"So start fresh."

"I have no other choice." He straightened a chair that had been knocked over, and sat on it as far away from me as possible. I felt like I was riddled with Goblin poison.

"I can't love you. I love someone else."

I didn't say anything. I stared at the floor.

"The Lord has a daughter who is the most beaut-" He suffocated the last word with a poorly forced cough. "This Fairy has caught my special attentions. It's not just her beauty that keeps me. When I was a boy, a foolish boy I might add, I almost drowned in a lake chasing after a frog." He laughed to himself. I wasn't entertained. "A young girl swam up from the bottom of the lake and pulled me down with her, but somehow, through her, I had the power to breathe while below the surface. We swam around the bottom of the lake for some time, chasing the fish and even the confounded frogs that nearly killed me in the first place. I swam after her through the seaweed, weaving in and out through the tall leaves, and when I spread two of them from my view, she kissed me." His eyes were glossy with nostalgia. I almost shot up and shook him awake, but he drew in a deep breath and continued. "I knew then that I loved her and always would. I followed her back to the tree and into her room. We laid innocently together that night in our wet clothes until the morning came and her father almost had me killed. She pleaded for my life, testing the tenderness of her father's heart. Ever since then I've been permitted to live in the kingdom but separated far away from the princess. Her memory always haunts me, and I can't forget about her." He lifted his head to look at me for the first time. "Last night, when I lifted you above me, you had transformed into her. It must have been a spell she put on you to remind me that she still exists. She is a bit envious, even though she knows well enough I have nothing to give to any other. She has my love."

His speech was so sincere and apologetic. He didn't mean to hurt me in any way and thought the best way to avoid causing me pain was to tell me the truth. I nodded my head and smiled in acceptance, though I couldn't avert the hankering of my heart. He could perceive this and apologized once more. I assured him that he had done nothing wrong and that it was my own fault. Hayden couldn't help but feel guilty for my broken heart as well as helpless to do anything to redress it. He got up to leave, but I called him back.

"I don't love you Hayden. I am just lonely and wanted a friend, and when we danced, the music enchanted me with spoony emotions. I'm sorry to have said something so thoughtlessly. Please forgive me."

His face brightened up a bit, and he flashed a quick smile.

"There is nothing to forgive. I would be honored to be your friend."

"Then it is settled. Friendship it is."

He winked in agreement and left the room with a lighter step. I lay back in my bed fully clothed and wept silently. I couldn't let him go to battle believing he had caused me pain. He could fight with the woman he loved as his motivation. It was my hope that he would evade death for the sake of his lover, even if his lover wasn't me.

He would fight to win over the king's approval, but if he fought with his heart and not with his mind, then he might forget the fear of death, which would ruin him. He'd be blinded with love for the very woman who had threatened me only moments ago. It hadn't really occurred to me until that moment that he had called her a princess. How could I love a man who loved such a wretched...*princess*? A real, horribly jealous princess who had captured the heart of her knight in shining armor. Unfortunately, I had selected him as my knight, too, but how could I compare to a genuine princess of the Fairies? It didn't really matter, though, of what title she was known by. What mattered was that in order to stay alive, Hayden must balance his love for the princess with his militant mind.

I thought about Hayden and the danger he would encounter on the battlefield. It concerned me that he would fight senselessly with rage rather than skillfully with focus. I watched in my imagination as he charged insurmountable numbers by himself with only his bare hands to shred apart anything that dared to stand between him and his beloved princess. Then I cringed as my vision flashed to the princess sitting high up in her tower, as ladies in distress are so wont to do. Her father, the king, reluctantly told her that Hayden had fallen in battle, and her screams were earsplitting, even for imaginary ones. They shook me into motion. Despite Hayden's forbidden heart, I was still connected to him in a way I had never been with another person. I didn't choose to love him, I simply did. I attempted to get up and advise him to fight with his head instead of his heart, but the pain that I had felt in my stomach the first night I danced returned tenfold, and I collapsed on the bed, yelling out for help. A very small servant Fairy that I had never seen before came to my aid and helped me to the physician. Somehow I drifted down long corridors as he floated beside me with wisps of a warm breeze blowing against my face. I knew he was talking to me, but it was impossible to understand him. Soon enough I was being analyzed by a doctor who put pressure on my stomach area. For the first time, a Fairy spoke directly to me in my language. The wind still blew as he spoke, but a low whisper echoed in my ear to tell me that I would be just fine. But despite this great news, his diagnosis was unwelcome and sickening. I was pregnant.

unheeded Advice

How? How in the world could I possibly be pregnant? The only conclusions I could think of were that a Goblin had found me alone and unconscious, or that Kruss had done the deed while he was torturing me. But if that was the answer, then the beast growing inside me was a Goblin child. I wanted nothing to do with it. Even if it was an *Hûvelle*, I wouldn't know how to care for it having never seen a decent mother figure in my life. In fact, I considered abusing myself to get rid of the monster thriving within me, but the thought of killing sounded horrid to me. Death was a serious matter after all, and I couldn't help but feel that I would be continuing on a vicious cycle of my mother abusing her child. There was so much confusion clashing inside me that I couldn't think clearly.

I had become despondent to the Fairy doctor and servant, even though they were very kind to me. I had only one person in mind to confess my doom to, but every time I asked for him, I was told he was occupied with training for battle. I knew what they told me was true, because the Fairies were too pure to lie, but I couldn't help but think that Hayden was lying in bed with his princess, proclaiming his love to her before he left for battle. Just as I was beginning to feel the ugly effects of envy, my heart's treasure slowly emerged from behind the door. He entered the hospital chamber cautiously, unsure of how to start the conversation.

"Congratulations."

"Please don't."

"It's joyous news."

"I've been raped, and now I'm forced to love the memory of it."

The terrible way I emphasized the word rape stung him and made him very uncomfortable. I would never tell him that the thing living inside of me was the creation of the very monster he was going to kill.

"What was his name?"

"It doesn't matter."

"Justice should be done."

"Stop talking about it."

He sat next to me on the bed, but I couldn't look at him. I felt even further away from him than the time he told me he couldn't love me. The distance between us was vast. In a strange way, I began to think that loving this child would make him jealous for my attention. Then it struck me that the child would be my own, and would most likely, out of instinct, have some kind of affection for me as its mother. Such a mixture of feelings was churning within me. I didn't want to think of it anymore. It was happening too fast.

"It isn't the child's fault. It's lucky to have a mother like you who will love it."

"Will I?"

"What do you mean?"

"How will I learn to love a child when I've never been loved?"

He dropped his head in embarrassment. I didn't mean his love, I meant my mother's, but I was too indifferent to tell him that. He removed himself from my side to sit stiffly in the chair.

"You are going to keep it, aren't you? The Fairies don't adopt the offspring of your type."

I shot him a look that charged him for his hypocrisy, but he didn't catch the meaning. He truly thought he was a Fairy. After having met the princess and then spending time with the doctor and his servant, it was clear to me that he wasn't of the Fairy breed. There was something imperfect about him.

"I don't need their charity anyway. Not all of us can be Fairies, either."

"I know that."

His last words were tainted with a condescending tone. I was nothing but a nameless gypsy girl again. Only now I was the mother of an illegitimate child; a monster; a repetition of my mother's disgrace. Only my child was not conceived willingly as I was. Despite my misfortune, I couldn't help but feel sympathy for the baby. I knew what it was like to feel unwanted.

"What a bitter sweet day. Today marks the death of a cherished human friend of the Fairies who was vanquished by his Goblin half, and you are going to be the mother of a beautiful child."

"Death?"

"And life."

"No, I mean who is dying?"

"I can't say his name before you because it was given by the Fairies and only the Fairies can use it, but he has been here since he was a child. I found it hard to visit him and say goodbye. He told me that sacrifices are soon to be made, but that the poison can always be sucked out of a wound. I just wish it wasn't him that had to be sacrificed. They are going to give him a poison that will put him to sleep. He will then pass over after twenty minutes of deep sleeping. The only poison that will come out of him is the Goblin blood his mother cursed him with."

It was then that I realized he was talking about the fiddle player. The only friend I had in the kingdom was going to die that day. For some absurd reason, my love for Hayden forced its way into my nerves and under my skin. I shuttered at the thought of him dying.

"Do you fear death?" My voice couldn't have sounded more childish.

"That's a blunt question, but to encourage your faith in me, no, I do not."

"I wish you did."

"Why is that?"

"If you feared death, you would be ready for it." My eyes fell to my hands in my lap. "Please be vigilant. Don't let love get in the way."

"Don't speak of love. It has been troubling me lately."

"Fight with a love and a fear."

"Fear will yield my courage and thus my sword." He spoke like a knight, alright. I admired him for his words, but his face was hardly a sage one. It was the face of a boy excited for his first fight. He had important things to prove to important people.

"No, fear will open your eyes. Don't underestimate its power."

"You are tired and speaking nonsense. What does a woman know of fighting?" He smiled as if to say, *don't worry, it will all be fine.* "I have to go now and ready myself for the war. I am proud to be part of the Fairies defeat over the Goblins." As he rose, I grabbed his arm to hold him back a little longer.

"All this talk of a war, and no one has told me when the big day is to happen. The only Fairy who willingly speaks to me is the doctor, and the only other human is to die today. The poor fiddle player."

"Yes, he is very dear to me. He will be put to rest as soon as the war begins. You see, we wait for the first leaf of autumn to fall, and that leaf will fall with the closing of a man's life. His sacrifice results in the beginning of our battle that will end all. When the leaf touches ground, then both sides are to prepare to charge. We shall meet the Goblins in a place near the lake where the princess and I met. It shall keep as a reminder to me." He stopped short so as to avoid an awkward moment. I couldn't get another word in before he was through the door and replaced by the doctor's servant who looked at me with knowing eyes. I felt completely nude before him as he observed my open emotions with pity, and then, as if lightening had struck me, I jolted from a fire that inflamed my stomach. A piercing pang caused me to tighten my body for ten seconds before I could release. Within that ten seconds, I knew that the baby inside of me was far from human. Frighteningly, and with utter disbelief, I heard a small growl vibrate from the depths of my loins.

Mikal O'Boyle

Impenetrable

Sleep became a stranger to me. The servant Fairies assigned to my bedchamber were to check on me during the three mealtimes of the day, but my appetite had befriended sleep. The servants reported this to the Lords, and I was watched carefully from then on. I was restless knowing that at any minute the fiddle player was going to be poisoned, and I was somewhere in the very same tree that the execution was taking place in. I was still a stranger to the various chambers and secret corridors of the tree, so I was tortured by my imagination that coerced the fiddle player into the worst possible room with no lights except the shining gold of the Fairy Lords' eyes. Despite their hospitality shown to the fiddle player, those gold eyes would never provide comfort to a human. They were too unnatural- well, as far as humans are concerned with nature. If I were to die, I would want to be somewhere in the woods with the snake by my side. I hope that I was enough of a comfort for the beloved snake when it was put to death.

Of course the thought of death brought about the thought of Hayden fighting and his unpredictable fate. I didn't know if he would actually consider my advice or simply ignore it. The battle was going to start at any moment, and it could possibly be the last time I saw him. The shock of the baby, the sudden attack of war, and Hayden's love for the princess were overwhelming me, but nothing possessed my thoughts more than Hayden's life. I had to make it clear to him how vital it was to prevent love from dominating his thoughts, so I requested his company yet again. It seemed to me that he hadn't completely taken in what I had said. All I could think about was this love struck man charging the battlefield without a hope in the world except loving the princess. Then, with that final thought, there she was. A massive image of her appeared in my head, or was it real? Her petite form expanded until her head was forced down by the ceiling. I lied in my bed with the cover pulled up to the bottom of my chin. Her beautiful human-like body blurred like breath on a mirror, and then within seconds she cleared up again into a dazzling cloud. Those golden eyes were glaring at me through the streaks of lightening that flashed within the ash gray cloud. Deep rolls of thunder were distant but very present. I shook my head and blinked my eyes deliberately to see if it was, in fact, a dream, but she was still there. Despite the intimidating surge of lightening only ten feet away from my bed, the whole scene was frighteningly magnificent. The princess must have sensed my awestruck stupor because she transformed back into that petite lady with golden eyes boring a hole in my forehead. I was no longer amazed, but utterly disheartened. What did she have to be jealous of? She was loved by the man I loved. I was no competition. She floated over to my side, dragged a very long and elegant finger up my arm, and then pinched me until I brushed her hand away.

"Your fiddle player has been put to rest, and I think it appropriate then that your foolish feelings for Hayden should follow him to the grave. I never liked the man anyway. He was of Goblin blood and reeked of it, just as you reek of decaying skin. It annoys me to be in this human state. The weight of this confounded *husk* is insufferable, but I should endure anything for my heart's treasure." She stared down at the sheets on my bed and talked as if I wasn't there. She paused for a few seconds, and then I watched as anger rose to her scowling mouth, then her crinkled nose, and finally her blazing eyes. It made me sick to see how appealing she was even though her hate was blatantly etched on her face. Her eyes spilled molten gold into mine. "As you apparently know, the leaf of initiation falls with the fiddle player's death. Autumn is the season of death, and so blood must run through our tree in order to color the red leaves. He has been made the sacrifice required for this war to begin. The first red leaf has fallen, thus initiating the commencement of the war and Hayden's march into battle. I come to you because I fear you have become a distraction to him after wickedly seducing him with your harlotry. He is only human after all, and though humans are not as pure as Fairies, Hayden is certainly unburdened by flaws most men would self-destruct from. Because of this, I find it my duty to warn you once more to distance yourself as far as you can from him, or you will undoubtedly beg for the mercy of such a death as the fiddler's. And believe me, you trollop, I will personally ensure that your punishment will be worse than that sentenced to a Goblin. Do not cross paths with me, snake killer."

Her pearly white teeth finally clamped her lashing tongue behind them. I could feel the sweat pouring down from my hairline. Without another word, she turned and floated out of my room. My heart pounded so hard that I thought it might burst through my chest. I don't know which was more domineering, the terror she had planted within me, or the fury provoked by her final accusation. How dare she call me a snake killer. I satisfied my cruel desire for her torture by imagining the snake biting her disgustingly pleasant face, which then blew up into a swollen melon. I wanted every bit of my strength to be exerted towards her physical pain, but the thoughts of pain once again brought me back to Hayden. He was preparing to fight while I was engrossed with the mental image of the princess's fat face. Even though she had threatened me with a merciless death, I was anguished over Hayden's imperiled life, and the helpless love struck girl within me opened my mouth like a puppet. I called to the servant who was ordered to stand outside my door, but having been temporarily dismissed by the princess, his response was delayed. I requested the company of Hayden, and although I emphasized how urgent it was,

Hayden didn't return my call until hours after I had sent it. He did, however, answer it, which meant something anyway. He appeared at my doorway sheepish and reluctant to enter. This was no time to be a coward.

"You wanted to see me?"

"Hayden, you have to listen to me. There isn't much time left."

"Today shall be the greatest day in Fairy history apart from the fiddler's death, though I do aim to avenge it. Maybe I will have my face carved in the walls of this tree." His face was as giddy as a child's.

"The battle can't be won in a day, you know."

"This is not a battle between humans or gypsies. The number of leaves in this forest signifies the number of days we've had to wait for this war, and after the falling of the first leaf, we are to march towards the ancient tree. The lake lies nearby. Even the Goblins know of this prophecy because Lord Yew decreed it the day he was poisoned. No one could understand what he meant by it until we found the Goblin who had murdered him. With the fall of the leaves comes the fall of the Goblins; only then can the leaves and the Fairies make a glorious change. If the Goblins succeed, there will be no more seasons. The leaves will fall all at once and winter will be continuous." His face changed from excited to solemn. "Only Goblins can survive the barren winters; no other living creatures can. They will begin to starve and by desperate measures will procreate exclusively with their own kind and eat the elders for survival. It is appalling and despicable, but that is the way of the Goblins."

Disgust was riddled all over his face, but he was nevertheless as handsome as the first time I saw him. I was tired of hearing about the laws of the war and decided that then was the right time to express my concern. If he had it fresh in his head before he charged into the front line of Goblins, then maybe he would heed it.

"Hayden, please take my advice into account. If you don't want the Goblins to destroy the world, then you *have* to listen to me."

"I can understand your loneliness. I had never loved until the princess rescued me. Before then I was an orphan, living in the world as an unknown to any human. I know she waits for me. We share a vision that our union will transpire when the war is done. Until then, I am also a prisoner like you, wandering the kingdom in anticipation of the war. I have prepared for seventeen years. Nothing can make me happier than this war."

A vision! I was worried that he thought fate would be all he needed. It was going to be harder than I thought to get my point across.

"If you want to see her again you have to fear the chance that you may not. Don't blind yourself with love. I am resisting that temptation this very second."

Hayden looked at me again with a sad expression in his eyes. I could tell I had made him uneasy with my last statement, but he didn't realize how he hurt me with his talk of the princess. I loved him, too.

"It is time that I leave. The King of Fairies is having a

feast for all the warriors. If I am not present, I will be considered an invalid. Don't worry about me. I will see you during the celebrations tomorrow. Try to rest your body. Your baby needs it."

Again he eluded my pleas. I was close to grasping his feet in supplication. I was desperate and distressed. I hated the princess who was going to lead him to his untimely death. She should be sentenced to death, charged with murder of the warrior Hayden whose only fault was to love her instead of me. She was his heart and I was his head, but he neglected the more important of the two. It was her incessant demands for love that fed him to the Goblins. I would have saved him, if only he would love me.

A Golden Opportunity

Drifting, falling, and rocking in a pendulum motion outside of my window was an autumn leaf. It was rusty orange traced with a sliver of gold. The veins of the leaf were of a blood red that webbed out to the edges of the fragile sides. It looked as if it would disintegrate before it even touched the ground, but instead, a soft wind plucked it from the branch, cradling it in midair just before it landed gracefully in a pool of rainwater collected in the roots of the tree. The leaf had spun in slow motion, as if time had yielded to its lamentable voyage of death. My tears fell freely. Nothing could be heard except the moaning of swaying trees and the sighs of martyr leaves dropping one by one. Soft crackling noises filled the air as the dying leaves were blown across the forest ground. Those that collided with the tree shattered into tiny bits before evaporating into nothing. Their impact was accompanied by a sort of tintinnabulation. The gold trace of the leaves glittered in the sunlight as usual, but the sun was hardly a welcomed friend. The morning was cold despite the sun's persistent rays. The smell of decay was in the air.

From my chamber window high up in the sky, I wept as a decorated wooden box was carried out before the army. Lush green ivy with golden edges was wrapped around all sides of the box. It was carved elegantly with symbols that I didn't recognize etched into the dark brown of the wood. The fiddle player's haggard face looked out at the army with soft, sad, timbered eyes. Eight floating Fairies lifted the coffin high in the air with thick vines that were tied onto either side of the wood. His muted fiddle was tied on tightly to the top of the coffin. Silence crept over the shuffling army. Every Fairy turned to look up at the fiddle player's coffin before wafting a soft breeze that chilled the tears on my cheeks, and then, without any more ceremonial services, the army set out towards the ancient tree. He was only human after all.

In the lead of the pack were the Lord's sons and subsequent to them was Hayden. His head was turned towards the princess I had known all too well, probably even better than Hayden knew her, but she was so beautiful it enraged me. Her dress enhanced every bit of her feminine qualities, which were so incredibly dainty and elegant. This feigned body was the poison that would kill Hayden. She watched him until the trees grew too thick to see through, then she faced her father silently and nodded. I, resolute on being less incompetent than the princess, thought of how to save Hayden's life, but to my dismay, I was as useless as the princess. All I could do was wait alone in my chamber for the news of his death. I wept bitterly to myself.

The servants came as usual to distribute my meals, but I didn't even look at the food they brought in. After the arrival of dinner, a loud banging pounded on my door, and I was jerked out of my lifeless state. A Lord of the Fairies stood face to face with me, glaring at me with his golden eyes. He had a servant Fairy translate for him, being proficient with the language of the *Hûvelles* after years of serving Hayden. His accent was thick, and his vocabulary was influenced by the *Hûvelles*, *which* made it difficult to understand, but we managed to communicate.

"Our Lord knows of your resounding pain and has come to ask for your forgiveness."

"Forgiveness?"

"He knows of your failure to advise Hayden as well as your strong feelings towards him."

I found it nearly impossible to look at the Lord who was expressing his sympathies to me through his servant. There was something too unnaturally powerful and mysterious about him.

"What's done is done."

"The Lord wants to redress the wrongs done to you by offering Hayden's hand in marriage. Both of you are humans, and you are a compatible wife for him."

Either the shock of this proposal or the symptoms of my pregnancy nearly made me vomit. Both were equally despised.

"Thank you for the offer, but I must decline."

"The Lord is not happy with your answer and demands that you accept."

I thought twice before telling him that Hayden was in love with his daughter, and so I thought up of a better reason.

"I am not human, I am half gypsy. I am of another race of people. My nation doesn't allow outside races to be married into the gypsy nation."

The translator let out gushes of wind from his mouth to tell the Lord what I had said. When he was finished, the Lord slowly turned to me and spoke in his Fairy language as the translator explained to me what the wind translated into.

"The Lord respects the laws of your people and would like to enter into conversation with you."

"I'm sorry. I don't understand. I am not fluent in Fairy."

"Close your eyes."

Not wanting to offend the Lord of Fairies, I shut my eyes as commanded. A deep rolling voice echoed in my ears, and I felt compelled to respond.

"The leaf has fallen and the Goblin's have started their march. The earth shakes with their heavy footfall. Unfortunately, what I have prophesied in a dream, you have also prophesied. Hayden may fall in battle. As the end of the war approaches, there is a chance that two soldiers will carry him back with a fatal bite from three

Goblins. In my dream three times he was bitten: once in the arm, once in the shoulder, and once in the neck. The last shall be the worst. The poison will be strong. He will not survive his wounds. I have never dreamed like this before and so I question its validity. That is why I offered him as a husband, but knowing how much you love him, it would be wrong for me to hide the omen of my dream. You will now have time to steady yourself if it should happen. "

"I don't want to hear this." My mind spoke instead of my mouth. It frightened me.

"You are a rational creature. The Diamond back has befriended you because you have experienced such hardships that have wizened you at a young age. You are not a stranger to fear or death, and you carry life within you though it was begotten in an unfortunate way. Your life seems to be a sacrifice in itself, but to what? The Diamond back who died by your side was a great ally of the Fairies. I can assure you that it is not you to blame for his death. His body has been found washed upon the shore, and now rests within the great halls of our deceased Lords. I can't help but wonder what drew the snake to you. You are a gypsy. Not a Fairy or a Snake, or any other eminent creature. Why did he bring you here?"

"I wish I knew the answer to your question. Everything I touch seems to wither slowly to death. How can I be of any help to your people?"

"We shall wait and see. I must go make preparations for Hayden's possible return. If it should happen, he will be admitted to the castle where he shall meet his end, but not before we attempt to save him. I will be at his side till the fight against the poison is done. This shall occur in ten hours time according to my dream. Be prepared nevertheless."

"May I have your permission to come? He has rescued me from the Goblins, and I haven't had the chance to thank him. I would like to do so before it is too late."

"Your reason is admirable enough. Be quick when the time comes."

I opened my eyes and watched as the servant and his Lord exited my chamber. Again, I began to cry. In my hour of hopelessness, I was overcome with despair. I wanted nothing to do with the Fairies, or Hayden, or this monster thriving inside me. All I wanted was death to come before misery could devour me. Then suddenly, I wanted Hayden again. I craved the sight of him. I jumped out of bed and fled to the window. Thoughts of leaping to my death crossed my mind. I took one shaky step onto the ledge, then another, and closed my eyes. The wind chilled the tears on my cheeks. Its rigor was refreshing on my heated body. I imagined Hayden standing below me, arms spread wide, encouraging me to fall into them. My fingers loosened their grip from the crevices in the bark. His smile was so genuine. He mouthed the word *please* to me. I looked down at him and was lashed by whipping strands of my hair. I returned the smile. His arms moved in a charade of a fiddle player, and the music began. He laughed, although I couldn't hear him. He was too far away. I spun on one foot on the ledge, not caring if I should fall or not. He would catch me if I did. The thought of lying in his arms was very tempting. I stopped dancing when the music stopped playing, and he opened his arms wide again. He pleaded for me to jump. I bent my knees, readied myself for the leap, but was shoved from the front at the very last second. Instead of landing in Hayden's arms, my body met with the hard solid floor of my chamber.

I didn't want to, but I opened my eyes. A green face was within inches of my own. Immediately I thought a Goblin had come to finish off what it had started. Kruss, maybe? I wasn't scared. I was thankful. His breath was revolting and I pushed him away from me. I couldn't believe what I was seeing. I actually rubbed my eyes to make sure what I was seeing was real. It was that same branch that had been swaying over my prison chamber in the Goblin tree, only this time it was so close that I couldn't possibly miss the face that stared back at me. Green oak leaves were painted on the face that was now in a state of panic. There were brown smudges to resemble the bark of a tree. Gold lines were painted on the edges of the leaves so precisely that it looked like leaves were glued to his face. I breathed out a whispered, "How?" and he responded with a huge, childish smile followed by some gibberish that I didn't understand. Realizing I didn't speak his language, he shook his head playfully, and then shouted out a name that rang in my ears.

"Girl!"

With that one word, I hated him. I attempted to get up, and he rushed to my side to help me.

"We've been looking all over for you! You're mother has lost her mind."

"Don't mention her, please!"

At first, he looked confused, and then he looked as if he understood.

"I, *ahem*, we, *erm*, well, I'm very glad to see you're okay."

His accent was strange considering that they spoke their own language, but they knew the gypsy language well. I had never met or even spoken to a Ginkgo before, and here was one, far away from my nation and choosing the worst possible time to find me. I do admit, though, that I was flustered by his message about my mother and all the memories that rushed back to me.

"I'm just fine. Better than I've ever been, actually."

"Listen, I'm not here to take you back. My family loved to watch you dance, and we saw everything that happened the day you disappeared."

I caught my breath. He knew I wanted to know. Without waiting for me to give him permission, he gave me the spiel.

"It was Rockel that caused it all! He knocked you down, and I think you were unconscious. I couldn't tell from where I was, but I figured you were because he grabbed the snake and he..." He hesitated and thought of a less cruel way to say the next word. "He ruined the snake. I wanted to wring him with my bare hands, but we're already the outcasts of our nation. I would have brought death to my family if I did anything. I have been just as much disowned as you have by our nation." The shame burned in his cheeks and flared the gold trim of the leaves on his face. "I don't know how to say this, but, Rockel abused you while you were unconscious. He..he..."

"Stop!" I screamed. I didn't want him to finish the statement. He didn't know how to anyway. The hatred boiled inside me, and then, it hit. The child within me was not a Goblin at all but a result left behind by Rockel's deviltry. It was worse than thinking it to be a Goblin baby. I shook violently with rage. A cool hand rested timidly on my shoulder. The Ginkgo's soft voice hardly soothed me.

"I'm so sorry for everything you have suffered. My family and I were searching for you because we wanted to offer you and your baby a place in our family. We used to watch you dance from the trees. We've always admired and pitied you. Your dancing brings joy wherever there is pain. Your child will be loved by us, as we all know how it feels to be abandoned. Please accept our offer. It would be a great honor for us."

My head was spinning from everything that I was taking in. Even the notion of abandoning my baby struck me hard. I suppose my child was nearly the same as me in regard to conception, and now someone wanted to love it. So many thoughts clogged my mind. The Lord of Fairies wanted me to marry Hayden, Hayden was going to die, I had been found by a Ginkgo, I was sexually abused by Rockel, the child within me was his, and now I being welcomed into the family of tree travelers. Foolishly, all I could say was what was on my mind.

"Hayden."

The Ginkgo didn't know what to make of my answer. He asked if I was feeling okay and helped me to my bed. I know that this boy was a stranger to me, and that everything he had told me brought more suffering, but there was something about him that connected me to him. He was a mix of home and where I was at the moment. I don't know what convinced me to do it, but I took in a deep breath and explained the whole situation to him. I told him how I was captured by the Goblins, how I was rescued by Hayden, the Fairies, the fiddle player, and finally the war. I expected him to console me when I had finished with the story, but instead he stood up rather abruptly with a severe look frozen on his face. I tried to puzzle out what he was thinking, but before I could ask anything, he was out the window. What good were the Ginkgos anyway?

the spirit of war

From the distant woods, I first heard what sounded like a ferocious hurricane blowing in the opposite direction of me. I could only assume that the savage wind was probably the war cry of the Fairies, because just after the big wind swooshed past me, I was assaulted by earsplitting screeches and guttural bellows which could only be made by the Goblins clashing into the stormy gales. My chest tightened out of panic, my lungs ceased to function, and all across my ribcage was a throbbing ache. I was trembling from head to foot and cringed whenever a shattering shriek could be heard. Every shriek brought to mind the three fatal bites that the Fairy Lord had told me about. I tried to calm myself with the thought that it was only a dream, and that the Fairy lord himself was uncertain of its credibility. I sat next to the window for an hour listening to the battle cries, the yelps of pain, and the bizarre sounds that I couldn't quite identify. For a moment it sounded as if a swarm of butterflies had burst into my room and were fluttering only inches away from my ear. I whimpered pitifully and almost simultaneously hoped that no one had heard it, but just as unexpected as before, the Ginkgo was back in my window with smeared paint all over his face. The lovely oak leaves were all ruined.

"Come with me. You're not safe here."

He held out his hand and puffed out his chest as if he was some kind of hero. How dare he tell me that there was a place safer than the Fairy Tree.

"I'll do no such thing."

The poor creature was momentarily crestfallen by my retort, but it soon changed into a determination that resulted in me being thrown over his shoulder in protest.

"Put me down right now! What are you doing?"

"If the Goblins storm the castle, they will torture you for the rest of your life. They won't kill you. They will make you their play thing, and I won't have the gypsy dancer treated worse than a slave."

His games of rescuing the maiden in distress were really getting on my nerves. I was so steamed at him that it took me awhile to notice that he was swinging from tree to tree and running with impressive agility along the branches. His balance was perfect. Then, with one big leap, he dove flawlessly through a big wall of leaves in a high tree and landed in a kind of circular room formed out of the twisted shape of the trunk. I had no time to concern myself with the natural surroundings because a bunch of wide-opened eyes were staring at me in wonder. I knew, without a doubt, that it had to be the Ginkgo family. All of their faces were painted like the oak leaves that were scattered throughout the room. I was speechless and beyond embarrassed.

"I have relocated you up here to keep you safe. This tree is not a main target of the Goblins, and from here you can see the whole war. My brothers and I have seen the way the Goblins fight, and I have told them how much pain they have put you through." He swept his arm to the side to indicate the brothers he was talking about. All of their faces were set like stone. One or two of them had expressions of pity oozing from their eyes. It was apparent that I was well liked by a people I had never really considered. Strangely, it touched me.

"We have decided that we will fight beside the Fairies. If the Goblins are the victors of this war, then they will eventually infest the world. They will stop at nothing as their demonic fighting and ravenous hunger for death has shown. Besides, to have a hand in such an important war will be an honor for us. All we ask is that you keep our sisters calm while we fight. Most of them are younger than you."

I looked at the huddled group of young girls perched on a branch that spiraled against the wall of the whole room. Many of them were crying, and others were still pleading the men to stay behind. The whole situation was such a shock to me that I couldn't even add my protest.

"We shall go now. The Fairies are in desperate need of our help. We can't wait any longer."

Mikal O'Boyle

With those final words, the Ginkgo brothers threw back some kind of dewy residue within cups made of rose petals that were prepared by the women, and then they climbed down the tree, one by one, and scattered into the field. I peered down from between the oak leaves and nearly fell out of the tree. The whole war was clear enough to see from where I was crouching on the branch. The Fairies were in big puffs of clouds and advancing towards the beast-like Goblins who were on all fours. Every so often I could hear them shouting in their demonic language. Whenever a cloud managed to swallow a Goblin, the Goblin would then disappear, but some of the Goblins ripped their way through the clouds, and bursts of gold would balloon around the spot where the Fairy once was. My eyes scoured the place for Hayden, but I couldn't find him. I saw one of the Ginkgo brothers land on the back on a Goblin, but he was easily bucked off and slashed to death by the Goblin's claws. Despite the sick feeling in my stomach, I couldn't rip my eyes away from the field. Puffs of gold were exploding everywhere, but I couldn't tell what was causing them. I was trying to narrow my sight in on anything that might look like Hayden, but with the Ginkgos mixed in, it was impossible to pick him out from the battle.

I was so caught up in spotting Hayden that I began to lean forward too far and nearly fell from the branch, but I was pulled back to an awareness when a shadow slowly crept over everything around me. It enveloped the whole tree that we were hiding in, and then it advanced forward, darkening all of the trees between the war and me. Eventually it reached the battlefield, causing some of the Goblins, Fairies, and Ginkgos to pause their fighting, look up, and see what it was. There was an intense quiet, and then suddenly the Fairies blew out another war cry, and somehow understanding their meaning, the Ginkgos began to whoop with them. I, like the soldiers, looked up to see what the big cloud was, and was taken aback by the thick flock of birds that happened to be blocking out the sun. Hundreds of wrens, hawks, robins and other birds started diving from the sky, jamming their beaks into the Goblins' bodies. They pecked at their heads, eyes, and ears persistently. It seemed to be pushing the Goblins back, but here and there a Goblin would snatch a bird from the air and shove it in its mouth. Feathers were drifting around the whole field, mingling in with the puffs of gold and the dying leaves. I could feel myself breathing hard, willing myself to climb down the tree and fight beside them until I rescued Hayden from this treacherous war, but my hands were glued onto the branch. I looked down at them to try to mentally pry them from the jagged bark, but it was no use.

I had only just looked down at my hands when an arrow struck the branch right between my two fingers, and within seconds, my hands were off the bark. I nearly lost my balance once again, but one of the Ginkgo women grabbed a hold of me, which steadied my frenzied attempt to remain on the branch. Once I was able to still my body, the girl, with her hand still firmly clasping my shoulder, pointed at a blue frog that had been impaled onto the arrow and was oozing some kind of slime. The poor thing was still trying to free itself from the arrow, but it wasn't long until its eyes closed and its tongue rolled out of its mouth and hung against the shaft. The corpse of the frog then bubbled and sizzled until the arrow melted from the acid-like goop exuding from the frog's mouth. The part of the arrow that held the impaled frog fell into a pile of leaves just below the tree, but the head of the arrow was still stuck into the bark.

I backed away from the opening in the leaves to stay out of arrow range. It didn't stop me, however, from searching for Hayden. With such horrible things as poisonous frog arrows flying around, his chances of survival were lessening. As I was looking for him, my eyes caught sight of a large net hastily proceeding onto the field by the Goblins. I looked harder, and as the net got closer, I could make out the distinct leaves of poison ivy. The whole net was made up of vines of black leaves resembling poison ivy, and it was being thrown over the Fairy clouds and Ginkgos. Although it only slowed the Fairies down, it did have an effect on the Ginkgos who fell to the ground rubbing their eyes and itching their skin. This gave the Goblins time to attack their prey, not with claws or teeth, but by shoving hemlock into their mouths. The Ginkgos, being forced to swallow the plant, would eventually start gasping for air before drawing their last breath. I had heard of this form of torture done by witches in fables, but to actually witness the effects struck my heart with fear and agony. I had never seen a poison act so fast. There is no telling what concoctions the Goblins had come up with to make their enemies suffer, but whatever this hemlock was reacting with caused a miserable, painful death.

The hemlock was only one way the Goblins were picking off their enemies. Others were holding Fairies and Ginkgos beneath the surface of the lake until they drowned. The cackling laughs from the Goblins whenever they made a kill were stomach wrenching. Then I saw one Ginkgo charge the field with what looked like a spear with a yellow and black frog impaled on it. It was none other than the very Ginkgo who had carried me to the tree. His passionate roar seemed to spur on the rest of the Fairies and Ginkgos, and myself, though my reaction was more the thrill of fear rather than the violent rapture of fighting for one's life. The long hair of the Ginkgos whipped behind them like shredded flags while their bare torsos were smeared with a mixture of dark paint and sticky blood that throbbed where their muscles flexed with every movement. Their frenzied attacks on the Goblins were far from human. The horror of the scene was very overpowering, and I found myself crying from the shock of so many deaths; so many horrible massacres that were executed by strangulation, disembowelment, devouring of living creatures, and other gruesome acts that are too disturbing for me to articulate.

Too many hours had gone by and Hayden still hadn't shown himself. After seeing so much mercilessness, I gave up the hope of his survival. The only human I would ever love, and who refused to love me, was lost forever. He may have never exchanged his heart for mine, but I could still have at least taken in small gulps of his presence. It would have ruined me in the end to have lingered behind him like a shadow, admiring him from the cold side of the firelight, but I could admire him nonetheless. To have had him nearby would have been just enough to keep me alive, but I would have inevitably gone mad from deprivation. Still, to have gone mad from a denied love would have been far more tolerable than suffering the suffocating depression of an eternal absence.

And while I was weeping and clenching my chest for the withering of my heart, a flickering second seized me, and I felt the smallest pulsation of joy for having sacrificed myself to something so powerfully consuming as love. I had loved. Truly, wholly, uncontrollably, and with the ultimate consequence of self-desecration, I had loved. But that foreign feeling of bliss was merely compulsive and fleeting because as I gazed the field with sullen indifference, I realized that my will to live was not gone, but simply less urgent as it had been. Should the Goblins conquer the Fairies, then so be it. Let them raid my corporal temple and taste my blood with the satisfaction of a wild hungry wolf. My shrunken heart would be a great disappointment to their enlarged appetites, but such false hopes would be of some consolation to me. So let them come. Let them finish me off. I have no need for a world blackened by sorrow, so let the Goblins do what they were created to do and tear the life from me.

The shedding

There is no feeling worse than the abandonment of a spirit from its body. I felt bitterly cold as I continued to watch the war for hours from the chosen tree of the Ginkgos though my body was moderately warm. Giving up my perched seat upon the surveillance branch, I decided to lean back against one of the many twisted arms of the trunk that partially formed the round room full of whimpering Ginkgo girls. I could just peek through the leaves of the branches to see a puff of gold here and a falling Ginkgo there. Now that I was a bit calmer, I could digest the war a little bit better, and I began to realize that whenever a Fairy was attacked, the gold puffs would burst. That could only mean one thing: the Fairy had died. At least they died in a shower of gold glitter as opposed to a heavy, cold, opened-eyed body that stared blindly at the world until dirt covered its face. Either way, beautiful or hideous, death was eternal, and so was Hayden's departure from my life.

I got an idea in my head then to try to ascertain who was actually winning the war. I had been so enveloped in my concern for Hayden that I didn't pay an ounce of attention to the outcome of the fighting. It seemed that there were far more Fairies and Ginkgos than there were Goblins, but the Goblins were tearing at the Fairies and Ginkgos as if they had all the reason in the world to think that they were the prechosen victors of the war. I narrowed my eyes on one Goblin who's familiarity would have once had an effect on me, but now when I looked upon Kruss as he slashed through a cloud that was once a Fairy, I felt nothing but hatred. There was no fear, just resentment. I wanted to kill him and leave the rest of the Goblins to the Fairies, but then again, I didn't care all the same.

I was beginning to lose interest in the war, in Kruss's advancement on the field, and the gaining of the Fairies, but then an odd sight brought me back to attention. A wave of something was rushing up behind the Goblins. At first I thought they were large dogs running on their hind feet, but within a matter of seconds, I saw the human faces of men, women, and children all sprinting up towards the Goblins. None of them had a single weapon. I was a little shocked to see people who hardly had any knowledge of the Goblins or Fairies come running full speed into battle with them. Perhaps the Fairies did have a chance to win. Some of the Ginkgo girls who had overheard me whispering the word "humans" to myself plucked up enough courage to look through the leaves and see the sight for themselves. They were all cheering with glee, as if the result of the war had been decided because a bunch of unarmed humans came running into the field of battle. I was more confused then relieved. What were they doing there? Then, with the most rough, drowning blow of a horn, the humans collapsed and began to convulse on the ground. I looked for the source of the horn, and there was Kruss, smiling smugly while holding a young Ginkgo in the air by the neck. As the Ginkgo struggled for air, the humans wiggled around in the grass only a few feet away from the Goblins. I thought of where I had heard the mention of a horn before and the fiddle player came into mind. He said something about a horn, and his mother changing, and then...

Just as I was struck by the revelation, the skin of the humans tore and ripped open like plastic bags, and out sprang more hideous Goblins to join the side of their kin. Despite thinking I couldn't feel any more disgust after giving up on Hayden, I did feel a great distress at the sight of human bodies being used as cocoons for slobbering, bloodthirsty Goblins. The poor Ginkgo, by this time, had been choked to death and tossed upon the ground like a dead animal. This seemed to have outraged one of the Fairies, because a deafening blow of wind blew, and a furious tornado made a straight path for Kruss, sucking in and flinging out numerous Goblins on the way. Two golden flashes could be seen from within the funnel of the tornado and instantly I knew it was one of the Fairy princes. His eyes were unmistakable. They were identical to the smoldering eyes of his father's. A flock of birds formed a V-shape behind him and a group of Ginkgos tried their best to keep up, but human legs don't compare to the gales of an angry storm.

Kruss, turning to face the oncoming attack, blew his horn again, and about fifty Goblins formed a kind of wall behind him. They climbed on top of each other, digging their claws into the Goblins below them. Kruss climbed to the very top of the wall and crouched as if waiting to strike with that same ugly grin on his face. I couldn't help but think that he had been waiting for this moment from the beginning of the war. As the Fairy prince edged in closer, the birds veered past him and dove right into the wall of Goblins, thrusting their beaks into the mutant faces of the enemy. A few places in the wall began to crumble, causing Kruss to sway unsteadily on the top, but his composure was unshaken. As soon as the Fairy prince was only a few feet away from the wall, Kruss leaped high into the air and dove straight down into the center of the funnel. The tornado lost control and began to whip about in a fury. Kruss and the prince were fighting in a place that was blocked off from the rest of the war, and only one of the two would emerge from the funnel.

Unwittingly, I pulled my knees into my chest and began to rock back and forth from excitement. This final blow could potentially end this bloodbath of a war. If only the prince would remain standing, then the Fairies could have the upper hand in the fight. The wall of the Goblins had completely collapsed and scattered bodies of both dead birds and Goblins polluted the ground. A few of the corpses were lifted in the suction of the rampant tornado and thrown miles into the sky. It was a horrible catastrophe to watch the limp bodies flying everywhere around the field. Most of the Goblins, Fairies, and Ginkgos stopped fighting to watch the incredible battle between the prince and Kruss. Something about the stillness around a chaotic fight to the death made the scene look so pitiful. The desperate hope of the Fairies was equivalent to the hope of the Goblins. They were like children watching their parents fight.

The tornado continued to lash about for some time until finally, and most despairingly, the funnel was reduced down to a transparent cloud, and within the cloud was the frail body of the prince laying helplessly in the large hand of Kruss. Both Kruss and the prince were marked all over with cuts and sores, but Kruss, with that never-changing smile on his face, showed his fangs to the Fairies before crushing the life out of the prince by closing his hand into a fist. He laughed until the spit gurgled in his throat, then he crammed the prince's body into his mouth, exaggerated the chomping of his teeth, and picked at them with one of his long claws.

The Goblins howled with laughter as the Fairies, silent at first, suddenly erupted into all kinds of storms. But there, in the midst of the field, was a human who looked like a ghost to me. He had to be a ghost. He shouted so loud that he drained out the rejoicing Goblins and even the booming thunder of the Fairies. With a sword held high over his head, he charged straight for Kruss, who was amused at the foolishness of the frenzied human. He signaled to the Goblins to let the human come through to him. It was clear that he thought another kill, this time without effort, would lighten the mood of his soldiers while crushing the morale of the Fairies. A little entertainment for himself, too, would be had.

As the human gained ground, I nearly burned out my own eyes from rubbing them so much. Tears gushed out of them, from happiness, from the traumatizing alteration of sorrow to joy, and from disbelief that it absolutely, without a doubt, could not possibly be Hayden running at full speed to his death only seconds after I experienced the piercing ecstasy of knowing he was alive. That ecstasy was short-lived as it quickly changed into pure horror when he was within only a few feet of Kruss. I stopped breathing all together.

Kruss pulled back one arm, ready to strike with a fatal blow, humored by this puny human running full speed ahead towards him. Hayden was charging so furiously that he didn't notice the Goblin soldier bounding out from the crowd in his direction, but the Goblin was stopped just short of his target as the ever-present Ginkgo who had been following me for so long tackled the Goblin to the ground and loosened the spear from his claws. The spear rolled directly in the path of Hayden's charge, and as soon as Kruss thrust his arm out where Hayden's face should have been, my heart's beloved stumbled over the spear, fell, and accidentally aimed his sword perfectly at Kruss's gut. I gasped when the sword plunged in, twisted, and tore out of the reptile-like flesh with blue goop flying from its blade. Everything had happened so fast. Kruss screamed out in pain and anger. With his last remaining energy, he dug his fangs into Hayden's neck as he attempted to get up. The fangs chomped deep into Hayden's throat, but it was only once, not three times. Nevertheless Hayden dropped to the ground only seconds after Kruss fell lifeless into a pile of mixed bodies.

I tried to gasp again, but my breath was gone from me. I stood up abruptly, terrifying the Ginkgo women. My whole body was unstable, and as I took a step along the branch, my knees weakened and I tumbled out of the tree. My life would have ended there if it wasn't for one of the Ginkgo warriors that was standing guard of the tree harboring his family. He caught me in midair, and said something about knowing I would react that way to Hayden's death. Everything was mumbled in my ear. Everything was blurred. Again I was over a shoulder and being carried along the branches of trees, but all I saw was a whirl of green, brown, and red. Then the dizziness stopped, and I was suddenly sitting on my bed in the Fairy Tree. The Ginkgo was on one knee before me, trying to pull me back to the world. He lured me into it by saying that Hayden wasn't dead, and that the Fairy lord was beckoning me. I hadn't even noticed that the Fairy lord was at the foot of my bed, patiently waiting for me to gain my sanity back. He urged me, through my thoughts, to follow him. There wasn't much time. Somehow the Fairies had whisked Hayden off the battlefield and into the Fairy Tree before I could even come to my senses. I had no idea how long I had lost them.

Mikal O'Boyle

I shot up off the bed and ran behind the Fairy lord and his translator. The Ginkgo stayed behind as he felt too unworthy to enter the chambers of the favorite human. I didn't question him or argue with him, I just followed the two out of my chamber. They moved swiftly through the hall past all the carved faces. I tried to design an eloquent speech in my head to deliver to Hayden on his deathbed, but before I could find a place to start, I was in his chamber and waiting impatiently. Everything was moving way too quickly. I didn't know how I had already entered his chamber without noticing which doors I had gone through to get there, but that was the least of my worries. Hayden, who I thought would be in the room, was nowhere to be found. They were still carrying him in from the battlefield. I didn't move from my spot next to the empty cot that was awaiting the dying soldier. Not just any soldier. Hayden. More hours. And more. I stared at my hands and thought of nothing but his handsome face. He was on the verge of death, and I could do nothing about it. Just as I began to hate myself for my uselessness, Hayden's crippled body floated in the room above six clouds of Fairies. They laid him before me. His face was drained of color. He was gasping for air.

I stared at Hayden imploringly, but his condition seemed hopeless. He was going to die. I watched as the King drifted over to Hayden's side, and I felt a soft breeze sweep the hair out of my eyes. He was whispering. I figured he was speaking words of encouragement to Hayden, but as the king was speaking, I saw a quick flash of a yellow glow. There was a firefly! Again I saw its flash, but this time it was in the depths of Hayden's ear. It lit up his closed eyelids then it found its way out of his other ear. Without thinking, I let it crawl into mine, craving the knowledge of Hayden's thoughts, but instead I was taken aback by the fear, excitement, and anger that was thrust into my heart. My vision, or what was once Hayden's vision on the battlefield, was limited to the two thin slits of Hayden's eyes that revealed a line of unfathomable creatures advancing towards me. I turned my head to my right, and there was the king's son slightly ahead of me.

He had stretched his form out into a slim, intimidating length that was grounded by a dark gray cloud rumbling like a distant storm. Sparks of light clashed within like lightening bolts, which were hardly being constrained. I looked up at his face and was horrified by the grotesqueness of his features. As he was only a young Fairy, he had not yet grown a beard, and in the place of a mouth there was only a deep black hole. The edges of the hole not only flapped in and out as he breathed, but it also drew in surrounding veins that were visible through the transparent skin. Their pulsation was clear enough to see the fluid surging through them. This could be seen only from the cheekbones down, and although the veins were only visible in that small portion of his face, their resemblance to a bloodshot eye made my stomach lurch. His cheekbones were much like that of a *Hûvelle*, but there was no nose to be seen. From his mouth to his eyes there remained an empty stretch of skin about a foot long, but his eyes were smoldering. The gold color seemed to bulge every so often as if it were boiling water. The strong resolution in this Fairy forced the skin above his eyes to gather, giving him a demonic semblance.

Afraid that he may become aware of my gawking, I turned my head back to the front again, but the sight was horrific. Standing too close for comfort were the Goblins. Thousands of them! All glaring and drooling ghoulishly. Unlike the composed lines of Fairies, the Goblins were jittery and shifted their weight, unable to restrain themselves from blurting out their ugly language with deep growls. They pushed, bit, punched, kicked, and even stabbed each other as a form of motivation. Some had teeth while others opened gaping mouths with a lolling tongue. The bodies were heavy with hanging limbs that swung clumsily. As they awaited the signal from Kruss to charge, they shot horrible looks with green eyes that changed to a brown sheen after blinking. My body moved without me telling it to, and I was caught off guard by my arm rising in unison with my fellow soldiers. My teeth grated top on bottom as my breathing began to shorten into sharp inhalations. I felt the urge to vomit but resisted it as the dirt below me began to swirl in a dust storm around my army. Just before the storm lifted over me, I glanced at the Ancient Tree in the distance, and without a second to lose, I shouted as loud as I could. My voice wasn't my own. It was Hayden's.

Everything he felt, I felt. The shout didn't last long as it was lost in the violent wind that bellowed in my ears. It was the battle cry of the Fairies. Then, *whoosh!* The dust storm instantly swept before us and took out the first two lines of Goblins who weren't expecting an attack so suddenly. Hundreds of Goblins flew back behind their lines from the force of the blow. In the newly opened space where the unfortunate Goblins had been standing, a large hideous creature ran on all fours across the front line. He shrieked something awful while slashing out at the lines with his nails. When he reached the end, he turned and looked directly at me with a hatred far more lethal than any *Hûvelle* or gypsy could muster. His green eyes were familiar. It only took me a second to realize it was the Goblin guard who had fed me goop covered in his saliva in the Ancient Tree. As if he recognized him, Hayden targeted the Goblin and made a path in his direction. I slashed out mercilessly, cutting down Goblin after Goblin. They shoved their face in mine, wagging their tongues mockingly while baring their fangs. Luckily the armor Hayden was wearing was too thick for the fangs to break through, although the pressure of their bites was very strong.

While I was on my death trail leading to the Goblin who attacked me, I heard a number of cracking noises. Sometimes it sounded like a tornado, but they didn't seem to phase Hayden. He continued to approach the Goblin without any hesitation. That's when disaster hit. Without any warning an image of the princess flashed before me. Before us. Hayden had stopped in his tracks, unable to find focus a couple feet in front of him. An enormous weight landed on him, and he fell heavily to the ground while claws tore through the armor on his arm. Two fangs sunk in to the bone with an excruciating pain. My lungs ached with the scream he let out, but it was shortly answered by the sound of a tornado.

I looked up quickly to see one of the Fairies standing above mm with a Goblin hanging on desperately to the edge of the Fairy's mouth. His whole body was being sucked into the Fairy's mouth, which was now widened to the size of a well. The suction was so strong that the veins surrounding the mouth grew in size, and the sniveling monster screamed before he lost his grip. Just like that, the Goblin was gone. The Fairy didn't waste time before he had caught his next victim. Hayden laid motionless on the ground stricken with terror from the Fairy's kill. It wasn't long before he broke out of his trance and started again on his mission to kill my previous acquaintance. The Goblins began to drop again, one after the other, landing in heaps upon other Goblin carcasses, but to my surprise, there were no Fairy bodies lying around. The only blood seeping into the forest ground was Goblin blood. The scent of death and filth was churning my stomach, but Hayden was unstoppable.

Boom! Again I crashed to the ground, but this time two Goblins had teamed together to protect the Goblin Hayden was adamant on killing. One of them had rammed into the back of my knees while the second one jammed its head into my chest. I couldn't breath for at least ten seconds. When my eyes finally focused again, I saw another Goblin being devoured by a Fairy, only this time the other Goblin that had attacked Hayden was scratching away at the Fairy's eyes. The first Goblin was swept away into the Fairy's mouth, but the second Goblin relentlessly dug its nails into the golden lights. Eventually the gold rolled out in tears down the Fairy's face where a nose should have been. There was a loud crack and the earth below the Fairy opened into a seam like an earthquake, depositing the Fairy's glittery particles into the hole. The crack ran far to the left and right, consuming the second Goblin and some of his allies along with him.

Hayden got up and ran as fast as he could away from the crack, but a female Goblin had injected her claws into his shoulder. She slowed him down a few feet, but he managed to lift her from his arm and throw her into the hole behind him. In the midst of a stampede consisting of both Fairies and Goblins, Hayden sprinted only a foot ahead of the expanding crack. Some of the Fairies sucked up as many Goblins as they could before they allowed the crack to swallow them with ten or more Goblins in their mouth. Hayden shoved some of the straggling Goblins in the hole as well, but the fingers of the crack eventually came to a stop. Many of the bulky Goblins were out of breath and lost their life due to their fatigue while the fighting resumed around them.

Not many Goblins stood between Hayden and the targeted Goblin anymore, and the aggression began to rise within his chest. He was bloodthirsty- a beast. He thought of nothing but killing this Goblin and would stop at nothing to accomplish it. Slash. Stab. Jerk. Swipe. One more Goblin and the target was his. The final Goblin stood no chance against Hayden as it slid slowly off the tip of his infinite blade. He panted with an exhaustion mingled with desire. Completely ignoring the aching in his body, he was wholly overtaken by the adrenaline rush that ignited his final fire. The Goblin smirked at Hayden as if he was a mere boy with a wooden sword. He picked his fangs with his claws and sucked at them with his tongue. Blue saliva oozed from the corners of his lips. Wiping it away with the back of his hand, he then sniffed indifferently before pointing his sword at Hayden. His challenge was answered by a forceful swing of Hayden's sword. For only a second, the Goblin's eyes betrayed his arrogance, but he quickly covered it up with a ghoulish smile. The fire blazed within Hayden, and he began to strike out blindly. A clang echoed within his helmet, but he kept swinging. Again the clang rang in my ears, but this time it faded away with the clear screams of war.

My helmet had been knocked off by the Goblin's sword, and within a second he had bitten my neck. He laughed while the poison began to flow, but my hand found the hilt of my sword. Its smooth gliding was halted by its entry into the Goblin's chest. The creature's laugh changed to a choking gargle. Blue oozed ran down my neck onto my chest. My body became too weak to move, my arms and legs were too heavy to lift, but after an agonizing length of time, I heard the fury of a violent tornado, and knowing that it was the prince who was struggling somewhere nearby, I found a impassioned strength deep within me urging me on to kill the Goblin who was fighting with my Lord.

My vision began to dim. It wasn't because Hayden was dying, but because the Fairies outside of my shared vision with Hayden were calling me back to the hospital chamber where Hayden's body was weakening. There were two Fairies floating on either side of me, demanding that I leave Hayden's body, but I clung on as tight as I could. One of them bore his golden eyes into me, purging my spirit out of Hayden's body. If I had stayed in any longer, I would have died with his memory. I opened my eyes startled, and instead of being inside Hayden's memories, I was standing beside his battered body, his pain still fresh within me.

Mikal O'Boyle

A sacrifice of Life

Hayden's face was purple and red, and his were eyes filling with blood. He couldn't remember who I was or what had happened. He was terrified of being in a room full of strangers. He was alone and in the hands of death.

"Hayden!"

"What are you doing? Let go of me. I don't know who you are."

"Yes you do. You've only forgotten because of the poison."

"I don't know who any of you are. Where is she?"

"Who?"

"The princess. Only love can cure me now. I remember someone telling me that just before he died. She is the one I love, she must come to me."

"Hayden, she can't come to you."

"She must! She will understand. I can't remember his face or name, but he told me love would save me. I have been made the sacrifice, and she the remedy."

He was mad with the disease. If only love could cure him then I could think of only one thing to do. The princess would never make it to his chamber in time, so I leaned in to kiss him, but he jerked his head away from me.

"What are you doing?" He shouted at me with a rage I didn't think he was capable of.

"I'm sorry."

"Someone help me! Death is coming quick!"

Fear took a hold of me, and I didn't have a choice. A horrifying thought came to my mind, and without thinking I put my lips to his arm, shoulder, and neck, sucking out from each a fang releasing a fluid that tasted like dead leaves and dirt. I spit out the fang and began to suck out the poison that flowed slowly through his veins. The more I pulled out of him, the dizzier I felt. He had already fainted, but I continued to draw the purple fluid from his body, spitting after each mouthful. After about an hour of removing the poison from his body, I noticed his former complexion had returned to his face and skin, and his harsh wheezing had settled into light sighs. When he was considerably better, I asked in an exasperated voice for the grass that had been placed upon my wound when I was bitten. In seconds, the wounds were covered with the grass that smelled of lemon and mint.

I couldn't stand much longer. The act of sucking out the poison had taken a toll on me, as did the exhaustion of fear. I fainted beside Hayden and woke up in my chamber tied securely to the posts of my bed. I assumed only a day or two had gone by, but when Hayden walked into my room, I knew by his improved state that it had been over a week.

"The Goblins have been defeated. I was told I played a big role in the war."

"Hayden. You survived the night."

"I have you to think for that."

"Why am I tied down?"

"I have some bad news for you. I'm terribly sorry."

"Am I to die?"

"No, but your baby has taken in all the poison you have pulled out of me."

I didn't know how to respond to this. I wasn't devastated, but I wasn't overjoyed. The idea of being loved by something began to sound comforting, but again Hayden had taken away my only chance at love.

"The venom that you inevitably swallowed went straight to your baby. The birth will be very painful. The baby will turn into a full-blooded Goblin within a few weeks. Goblin babies grow much faster than human babies, and they are far more aggressive in the womb. We have tied you down in case you should by chance catch the disease and become a Goblin yourself. I'm glad to see you have escaped the terrible fate so far, and I hope you remain yourself. The baby must be killed immediately however, which is another reason you have been tied down. The Fairies are afraid you will try to hide the baby from us. Understand that it will put an end to you as well as the peace we have finally won. It is the origin of another Goblin attack. Unfortunately it has to be this way."

For a moment, I regretted the fact that my child would be so easily sentenced to death, but the thought of the child forming into a Goblin eased any doubts that I had. It wasn't a baby at all. It wasn't even human. My mind then wondered to things of more importance- things that actually weighed me down.

"Hayden, I'm sorry for trying to kiss you. It was rash, and I thought it was the only way to save you."

"I don't remember you doing that. To be honest, you are a stranger to me. The amnesia has affected my memory greatly. All I remember is the princess telling me to fight with my head as well as my heart. I ignored her invaluable advice and almost died because of it. She said this out of love for me, but I was so blinded by my affections for her that I didn't hear a word of it. Her words only prove her deep adoration for me. She is a sensible woman, suitable for war, but I would not have her mar her beauty."

He chuckled to himself cheerfully, unaffected by his near death experience.

"We should all be thankful for her." The sarcasm in my voice was obvious to all except Hayden.

"After you sucked the poison out of me, I was able to join the army again. I slaughtered many Goblins and ran my spear through the two Goblin princes as the sun rose. Within a day the war was won, and our peace restored. By the end of next autumn the Fairies will be reinstated in the

Ancient Tree. It is a happy day for the Fairies."

I hated him with my whole heart because I loved him just as much. I couldn't stand to look at his face, so I told the servants I was too tired to admit his company. When the baby was removed from my womb, the Fairies gave it the same poison they gave the fiddle player out of respect for me. Again I felt a strange tug from within my chest at the thought of the quick denial of my child's life. I couldn't help but think that it would have been like the snake to me. If it didn't love me, it might have at least cared for me. If I hadn't kept it, the Ginkgos would have, which was an uplifting thought, but because it was a Goblin, there was no hope for it. The feeling of a lost child only enhanced my depression, and I told the King of Fairies that I longed for home and that my nation needed me. He pretended to understand and respect my wishes, but the fireflies informed the Lord of my true incentive. I couldn't exist where the deprivation of love would torture me, and I was released without saying goodbye to Hayden. I had repaid the debt I owed him. That satisfied me enough.

Alone at Last

There was nowhere for me to go, and I would never be able to find my gypsy nation anyway. They were a nomadic people, and so it was in my blood to constantly be on the move as well. Having stayed in the kingdom of the Fairies and awaited the death of my Goblin infested baby was difficult. Not only had I been confined in the kingdom but I had also been given strict orders to never leave my room. After I healed from the pregnancy, I went directly to the lords and asked permission for my departure. They unanimously agreed that it was best to grant me my freedom as I had done them no harm and proved to be a survivor of many hardships. To cause me any more pain would have been cruel, and so I was free to leave.

The Ginkgo seemed to understand my pain after having lost my child and respected my decision to be left alone, although sometimes I swear I see a branch swaying in the most bizarre places. As for my heart's beloved, I never saw Hayden after our last discourse. I didn't want to, and I hoped never to see him again. To ensure that he remained unaware from me, I boarded a ship docked in the harbor and hid until the crew set sail the following day. They discovered me under the bed in the captain's quarters and agreed to let me off at the first sojourn. One of the shipmates asked me how a fourteen-year-old girl could ever leave home. I replied that I didn't feel fourteen but rather thirty years old, and that I was an orphan. He shook his head in pity and didn't engage in conversation with me anymore. He was a father of six children and couldn't stand the thought of his children being orphans.

The ship finally let down anchor after four months of traveling. The captain, who had an animosity for me since my discovery, harshly shoved me down the wooden ramp. He was relieved to get rid of a burden like me. I landed prostrate on the sandy shore with ten little toes wiggling in my face. A little boy of about seven years was covered in ragged cloths and asked me for some food. I told him to get lost, but he stood still and waited for the rest of the crew to exit the ship. I got up, walked past him, and wandered around the sleeping village. All the streets were deserted so I was free to go where I pleased. My main concern was shelter, and upon finding a small alleyway with a neglected canopy, I crawled under it and fell asleep.

I arose the next morning, stiff, sore, and ready to vomit. I stretched my legs and kicked something soft. It was the little boy from the night before lying just outside of the canopy's overhang. I realized I must have raided his home and left him to sleep outside like a dog. He hugged a loaf of bread tightly and didn't wake up after my kick. A *Hûvelle* walked by the canopy and shook his head at us, tossing a few coins in my lap then walked on. This happened a couple more times before the boy awoke and saw the shining coins that lay between us. I told him to look despairingly and latch on to my waist. He did so, and as people walked by I would tell them the tragedy of our parents' death and the happy ending of our reunion. I could see in their eyes that they wanted to know our sad story, but the concluding meeting of brother and sister consoled them. It was the devastating tragedy of our parents' death that grasped them and induced them to empty their change purses. Just like the shipmate, they were moved by the thought of their children becoming orphans and being cursed with the life that my adopted brother and I were left with. We played them for fools.

As most of the *Hûvelles* had already heard my story, I began telling a more adventurous tale, twisting and turning the whole shape of it until it melted in my listeners' ears. Sometimes I would get tired of telling stories and would dance for my audience while the little boy collected the pity change. The boy was useless for the most part now that everyone had known his heartbreaking history, but I began to believe the fairy tale myself. He never seemed like a brother to me, but he did become a kind of pet. He was obedient, loyal, and he was company. I didn't need him for anything else. He relentlessly asked me about my life and the hunch in my back, but I never told him and never would. He said I danced like the gypsies he had seen once. I probed him about the gypsies, asking what he knew and saw. He said he could only remember one story that frightened him so much that he would never see or talk to a gypsy again. I asked him to repeat the tale, that maybe I had heard it and could tell him whether it was true or false.

"It was about a beautiful gypsy woman who lost her daughter to the sea. It was rumored throughout the tribe that two of the gypsy children had hated the girl because she was so ugly and mean. So they locked her in a box and put her on a ship. When the mother asked around for her daughter, no one knew what had happened, but the two children would constantly sing a tune about the girl becoming worm's food. Consequently, the rest of the tribe's children joined in the song and would harass the mother about her child's death. One month later, the two children went missing but only for a couple weeks. They were soon found in their beds where the murderer had later placed them. Their corpses were swollen with water and buried under piles of squirming worms. It was easy to solve the murder, and the mother of the missing daughter was boiled alive in scolding hot water."

At that moment I wanted to be with my mother in the scolding hot water. I am already disfigured like she was and scarred by an unnatural pregnancy. Now that I know she is dead I feel completely and irrevocably alone- like I am shut up in my box with no chance of escape. I am the only skeleton hanging from the noose, swinging back and forth with the creaking of the wooden beam. Sometimes I hide within myself, ignoring the boy and the world around me. During the day I dream that Hayden woke up from the princess's spell and set out to save me from my self-destruction. I dream that I followed in my mother's footsteps and became the most gifted dancer of my nation, and my people flocked to me with offerings of their friendship. I dream the snake came back from the dead and stayed with me forever, but each time I wake up, the reality of my situation overwhelms me with gloom. Eventually I will pull out from this abysmal despair and begin retelling my stories in the day, but for the moment, I can't avoid the dreams at night that drag me into happy hallucinations then jolt me awake into reality. I am still hunched. I am still alone. I am still unloved.

I asked you from the beginning not to ask of my name because it is one that summons up a painful memory, but since I have retold my history to you thus far, I will tell you where it comes from. The Fairies gave me a name in honor of saving Hayden. It is a name given by the Fairies and therefore only the Fairies can use it, but I will tell you what it means. I was bequeathed the name Snake, though more pure in the Fairy tongue, in honor of my diamond back friend who died by my side. I find this name far more appropriate and deserving than the title *Girl* that my nation had attached to me. Unfortunately, there are no Fairies around to fill me with the pride that I exalt in upon hearing my name, but there is no reason for me to expect fate to be kind. Fate has made me its victim.

I am now sixty years old, and I have been telling stories in this village for a long time. The little boy I spoke of has become a member of a crew, returning every six months to come visit me. My loneliness deepens with his absence, but I'm sure you find it hard to believe that a woman with such a relentless past could experience a lower level of despair. Everything I tell you is true, however, and I've never altered a word of my story once. I tell you this not for your money or your pity, I tell you because I want you to believe it. That is part of a gypsy's trait- to never let a false word slip from her lips. Have a look at my hunch, or wait a few months to make acquaintance with the boy who is now a shipmate. He will validate my coming here and tell you that I was thrust off a ship before his eyes. He would never lie to a stranger; he is too sweet a boy. You must trust in my words because a gypsy always tells a true story, no matter how unfortunate the ending. I swear it.

THE END

CPSIA information can be obtained at www.ICGtesting.com
Printed in the USA
LVOW08s2221210214

374705LV00005B/502/P